The Book of Rapture

NIKKI GEMMELL

The Book of Rapture

FOURTH ESTATE · *London*

First published in Great Britain in 2009 by
Fourth Estate
An imprint of HarperCollins*Publishers*
77–85 Fulham Palace Road
London W6 8JB
www.4thestate.co.uk

Visit our authors' blog: www.fifthestate.co.uk
Love this book? www.bookarmy.com

ISBN 978-0-00-730035-8

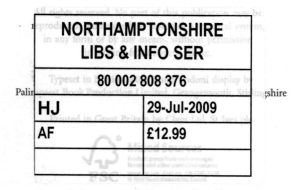

To A, L, O and T

My wild love

Introduction

What we know, and what we don't,
about this mysterious document

The Book of Rapture was originally written in Latin, a universal language unused in this day and age. Why? We can only speculate. Did the author want to obscure, to some extent, the content from her captors? Did the author want to mask her identity and indeed nationality? Did the author resist the idea of her words being pinned down – and thus marginalised – by place, religion or date? Indeed, the text could have emanated from any number of countries over the past century, from communist Eastern Europe to rightist regimes in South America to dictatorships in Africa or South-East Asia. It is obvious that names have been changed; all we can conclude, with precision, is that a woman wrote it.

It was handed to the Chief Philologist of the British Library by a man who described himself as a social worker, with an interest in children. On the front of the handwritten manuscript, bound in string, was a pink slip of paper with Prisoner Number 57775 typed upon it. The pages themselves bear the markings of a remarkable journey. Some are torn, some are bloodstained.

The social worker explained that a child, who was with two others, had lifted the manuscript from her suitcase and had handed it to him 'with an arresting gravity'. When asked what the bundle was, the youngster had replied, in a whisper, 'It is the words that roar.' The man said that the girl herself did not read Latin, and this in itself is a mystery: was the child aware of the document's contents? Was she connected to the protagonist, or indeed the social worker? Are they – as has been speculated – the father and daughter within the text?

We do not know, because despite strenuous efforts the man, institution he worked for, and children were never traced. They have all proved as elusive and mysterious as the document itself. There is one other fragment that was related by the social worker as he handed over the document. He said the child told him, 'Please don't forget us,' echoing, of course, the words in chapter 100 of the text.

The Book of Rapture is a historical enigma. Its author, provenance and audience are unknown to us. Scholars have striven to pin certainties upon it but the debate provides progressively less consensus every year. The honest and defeatist truth is that it is undatable and unsourceable.

It is of our time, and timeless. Near the beginning, and at the end, is the haunting statement, 'Now is the time when what you believe in is put to the test.' *Rapture* is a document of mysteries, just like the central question it asks: is all that is left a god of mysteries? It explores with an almost mythical quality the conflict between science and religion, notions of theological sacrifice, and a woman's impotent – and potent – rage. It asks that vexed question: if science does succeed in destroying religion, what moral code do we then live by?

There are no certainties. What journey has this document itself gone on? And its protagonist? Since its discovery the text has been debated over, fiercely attacked and fiercely defended. It is important for philologists to admit that we cannot place it precisely. Let us say, instead, that it is a document of the human condition. Many of its themes, surely, are as old as humanity itself.

Professor A.R. Bowler, University of London

Prisoner Number: 57775

It is the mark of a narrow world that it mistrusts the undefined.

JOSEPH ROTH

1

So. They are in there. Your children. Close but you cannot reach them, talk to them. In a room they've never seen before. That they've just woken up in. And the three of them are like tiny wooden boats in a wind-tossed sea, swivelling, unanchored, lost. Now a key has come. Rattling hard on the other side of the door; the only way to escape. You haven't a clue who's on the other side. Neither do they. The rattling's brisk, curt, adult. You feel like your heart is being compressed into your chest, a great weight is upon it, breathing is hard. Your middle child's knuckles are pressed into his temples, you can read his screwed-up face – this could be good-strange but he doesn't know – he's too huge-hearted for this. Always glass half-full but the dark side of optimism is trusting too much. Not his brother or sister. They're too aware for trust, they're thinking the worst. *Question everything*, you've told them all, so many times, and that's exactly what they're both doing.

The fear plague has come, it has hit.

And all you can do is stand here helpless in the wings of these words with your greedy, voluptuous love haemorrhaging out.

Nothing evolves us like love.

❦ 2 ❧

Nothing evolves us like love. Five words. From your husband, in a whisper, from one of his books. His collection of books. The only things with you in this room of held breath, his gift of a bookshelf he was curating for his children. Tomes on every religion. So each child could one day, eventually, decide for themselves. Be a student of all of them or none. That was the plan.

Did he slip them into your suitcase at the last minute? His final surprise? Once, long ago, it was Mickey Mouse stickers all through your address book and notebook. His silent chant, in gleeful sing-song – 'I'm he-re' – that little giggle of impishness from your perpetual boy up the back of the class.

But now this. A dozen or more books. All that's left from your past life. All that's allowed. Each volume fanned with dog-ears on the bottom corners. You know his method, he's had it since university: each turned-up page will have a tiny indentation down a phrase of interest, a thumbnail scratch to remind him to take note.

Nothing evolves us like love.

The first marked words you have come across. A key to unlock all this? A code? You hate uncertainty more than anything, he knows that. Okay. Okay. So. You will stitch his snippets into a quilt of words, trying to glean sense. Your little patchwork blanket in this place. Yes. You need to busy yourself up; need order, industry. To keep you going, to anchor you.

You cannot hear outside. You've always had it close. It's

nowhere now. Where are you? So, your quilt of words. To keep you warm in this room. To brew light. Little rituals, little certainties. Words from your Motl, your Man on the Loose. Sending you a message from God knows where.

Trust me, Motl said, trust. Those were his last words to you. Trust.

Now is the time when what you believe in is put to the test.

Be still.

∽ 3 ∾

You met over Bunsen burners. Wearing white coats. Star students both. Married, louchely, young. Had three kids. A girl, then twin boys. Lived a frugal life, five people in two bedrooms, but it worked: the Giggle Palace was your tiny flat and it was crammed with books and laughter and light. Your husband and you egged each other on at the vanguard of genetic research. Then you both received the summons from the government. And everything sparkled right up.

Project Indigo.

World-changing. War-changing. A weapon of mass destruction that would blaze your names into the history books. So audacious, shocking, astounding was the idea. The thought of it once made you smile and lick your lips. That every person on earth would one day know of you, for nothing like this had ever been dared. The *grandeur* of it. You, the only woman in a team of four. A top-secret coven, searing your place into scientific history, the delicious sweetness of that.

Then Motl dropped out.

'We're getting way above ourselves, my love.' He cufflinked your wrists into a grip that wouldn't soften. 'What moral code are we living by if we're living beyond religion? We're not working within any known ethical framework here. Are we? Eh?'

'Oh, you.' You nervously laughed. 'Humans can be moral whether they believe in a god or not. It's called evolution, little

4

boy. We've outgrown the religious approach to the world. All that, pah' – you batted the thought away – 'it's all lies and creaky myth.'

'I'm just not sure, wife, that it's possible to create morality in a vacuum. By putting humans first, before a god, any god. There are lots of tasty examples from history of attempts to put people – just one, or an entire race – first.'

'Religion, *husband*, is an affront to free will.' You whipped your hands free. 'It challenges reason, and intelligence, and common sense.'

'Look, I've given this a lot of thought.' His finger pressed in his lips, something big was coming up, 'As I've aged there's a . . . retreat . . . from certainty. That's the only way I can describe it. And I do *not* think science is capable of shaping a new moral code – or a better one.'

'Leave the project then. I can do it without you.'

He did. He resigned. Becoming, in an instant, your man on the loose. The house husband who raised the kids while studying, loosely, for yet another PhD. You became the bread-winner. Project Indigo, your stunning baby, saw to that. You weren't letting the dream go, oh no, or the boys' club that revolved around it. To the outside world you were engaged at the forefront of research; benign, for the good of humanity, and you were happy to keep it at that. But every day – magnif-icently, consumingly – you craved your baby's illicit potency. You'd wear your Vivienne Westwood Sex shoes and fuck-me underwear under the white coat because the whole vast and greedy ambition of the work sexed you up. It consumed your life. And then you'd go home.

To the suburb everyone else wanted to live in. To the sprawling house of room upon room and lonely beds in far corners never used. Rented and furnished by the project and you touched the luxury of the place lightly, didn't live within it but alongside it, distracted and buzzy and chuffed. To a garden vivid with insistent life. To the children changing physically with all that space to run around in, becoming fleet. To the gardener, the housekeeper, the PA's PA. To the nanny and her whims but you were at the crest of global fame so be it. And terrorism back then: older kids with slingshots in the next street. Another world, another country, another life.

There shall be faces on that day radiant, laughing and joyous; and faces on that day with dust upon them, blackness shall cover them.

∞ 4 ∞

Your youngest is crumbling. Here comes Mouse's scream and your body flinches as he opens his mouth but Soli, your daughter, your eldest, holds her hand high, stopping them all quiet. 'Sssh,' she hisses in a voice she never shows to you. You press close, trying to will your love into them, spine them up. Mouse pushes into his big sister, needs her authority close. You know his heart, that little boxer inside him jabbing away at his skin – punch-*punch* punch-*punch*. Mummy, he mouths and your palm slams to your lips and you will them all strong, trying to solder calm into their skittery, swivelly backs. But little Mouse, his heart's ramming so hard, it's like when you forced him into swimming lessons too young and he screamed at the water's edge and as you held him tight you could feel his terror battering your chest; it was like some wild unearthly thing in his ribcage, so huge, vulnerable, fast. My God, you thought, he could die here, his heart might just . . . freeze. With fright.

The doorknob turns. All their breathings stop, as crisp as an orchestra they stop—

Then . . . *nothing*.

The door doesn't open. Doesn't do anything. The person on the other side is . . . gone.

A vast, pluming silence. And your three children: ppfffft, like wilting tyres softening down.

Now they've got to work out how to get away from this place. *Fast*. Can they do it without you?

'Trust me.' Motl's last words to you and you had to surrender to them.

Will see your children if you resume the project? Will you see your husband if you give over your secrets? Will you be freed from this room to eat them all with kisses? You hold the key. You do not know what is going on. No one talks, no one answers your questions. They hand you food through a hatch with eyes as dead as models' on a catwalk. You don't know who they are, what side they're on, what authority they're working for. Or where your children actually are. Or your Motl. All you have to touch, to smell, kiss, are his books; his secret missives in a thumbnail scratch.

Do not be afraid; you are with them.

❦ 5 ❧

'Our country's smelling of blood.'

'Why, Mummy, is it hurt?'

Motl and you had swivelled your heads to the cupboard under the stairs, to the voice-that-couldn't-help-itself coming from inside it. Mouse. Of course. 'Stop tuning in, you,' his father had remonstrated, 'you listen too much.'

You demanded the notebook your boy was filling up.

Well, well. Like a forensic detective he'd been recording all the new chatter about him, trying to work his new country out. You sighed. This needed a talk. Because yes, your nation was changing. Battening down the hatches, locking the rest of the world out. And it was becoming increasingly uncomfortable for the likes of your family. The way you lived was seen by others as lost and bloated and wrong, people like you were being stained by the religion of your parents and grandparents, your reluctant past was becoming nigh on impossible to shake off; like some homeless dog endlessly tagging along and butting up close.

'It's a fear plague, isn't it? It's coming.'

Your little boy's deep brown eyes, that went on forever, implored to be treated as an adult.

'Sssh, it's okay, it's all right.' As you held his silky head to your hugely beating heart.

All the empty soothing platitudes and how you hate them now. Because they believed them, they trusted you. And all you are left with now are the books, all that male strut and threat you've always dismissed with a snort. Never really looked at. Carefully you sew your quilt, carefully you sew, writing in the dead language you haven't used for so long, stretching your brain like a pianist's fingers over keys, untouched for decades, and it all flooding back. Sew the words, sew.

One religion is as true as another.

∞ 6 ∞

Over those galloping days of regime change the writing in Mouse's notebook increased. And the lure of Project Indigo began to sour. You'd signed up in the ruthless ambitiousness of your pre-children days, when motherhood was dismissed as a weakness, a giving in. But suddenly, in your late twenties, your periods became heavier and your body was held hostage to a new, monstrous phenomenon: baby-yearn. *Insisted.* And with children all your job-hunger just . . . softened away . . . like water spilt into sand. You struggled for so long to come to terms with it. Fought, hard. But motherhood slowed you, loosened you, evened you; addled you with tiredness and forced you to relinquish control. Eventually, you gave in. Children won.

'Thank God you've seen the light,' Motl said. Because he didn't feel safe any more with Project Indigo hovering about you; it was getting too jumpy in this new political climate. There was no consistency, neither of you liked what was happening around you; your country was riven with ancient rivalries and the situation seemed impossible, hopeless, intractable; never to be untangled; never to be bathed in forgetting and peace. The different ethnic groups had fought each other since time began and long memories and grievances had fed a vendetta culture and now everything was escalating to a dangerous extent; there was extreme nationalist rhetoric on both sides and your project was an explosive secret at the heart of it and it was best to slip away, disappear, forget.

So. You both decided on a new word. *Measures.* Your life would now swing like an ocean liner changing its course. The plan was to flee the sparkly new house until your country worked itself out. You'd all vanish in a night. The past wouldn't find you any more; you'd be too far away, too remote. You'd find an old wreck of a place in the middle of nowhere, where your family could weather any trouble flat-broke but far away, and safe.

You whisper that lovely word now.

Safe.

It's the most luminous word in the world, don't you think?

When making your choice in life, do not neglect to live.

∞ 7 ∞

Their doorknob's now rattling like someone wants to shake it right off.

A bang.

The door shudders. Everything is quiet. Not good quiet, creepy quiet. And the only noise is their jagged breathing too loud and they can't still their breaths as the three of them stare at that feral door wondering what on earth it's springing on them next. And you. Watching. Glary with guilt and help-lessness, riddled with rangy light. Your middle child, Tidge, is bone white. He clutches his chest, at a mothy flittery some-thing inside him batting away like a sparrow in a room, trying to find sky, get out. He reaches across and finds his little brother's hand but Mouse's pulse is leaping like a flea on steroids and Tidge winces, he's not good with blood and bone, he can't hold any more, lets go. 'Thanks, dude,' Mouse says, soft, 'great.' So his siblings can hear it but the person out there can't.

His wiliness constantly surprises you. That guile of the third-born. He can't compete physically so he's always competed with something else. Cunning. Irony. An aware heart. One day perhaps he'll run rings around his brother, you've always said that, but is he wily enough to get out of this? Can any of them? You can't help them, they're by themselves.

13

Everything ahead, wide open, like a bull on the loose.

*Work out your own salvation with fear
and trembling.*

8

When they woke up they were in another world entirely. A room pale all over as if a big milky tongue had licked it into stillness. With a hush like all the silence of the world had gathered in it. A congregation of quiet. As if the space had been waiting patiently, just for them, its breath held like a morning frost.

'This room doesn't like us,' Mouse whispered.

'We have to get out,' Tidge.

'We can't.' Soli. Miss Practical, raising her eyebrows at the door.

'It doesn't like us,' Mouse repeated.

As fear tiptoed up your spine like a daddy-long-legs.

These are the unbelievers, the impure.

❦ 9 ❦

Salt Cottage. That was its name. The little house purchased in
the name of a friend who would never be traced back to you.
Dirt roads faltered to it, lost their will and almost petered out.
'No, no, no,' Mouse protested on first seeing it, twisting his
head as if possessed. He didn't do rural, didn't get it. But the
land had kidnapped your heart. It was near to where you'd
grown up and the sanctuary of home, the thought of its embrace
as the world darkened around you, stilled you down.

'It has the same sky.' You twirled under it and laughed. 'Trust
me.' You bent to your scowly little man – 'it'll worm its way
under your skin, just you wait' – and a tickle under his chin
unlocked a smile. Just. Because for you, this place was like
striding into calm. You were in control again, you'd grow quiet
here, relax. And if you were happy the kids would be happy,
you'd learned that.

The cottage clung tenaciously to the farthest edge of your
country, a tiny stone blip among the endless squally chatter of
sea and sky. The approach was impossible by sea: jagged rocks
and furious waves deterred any boat. Seagulls poured down to
daily scraps and the wind could blow a dog off a chain, but
after six months of hard work a new roof sat snug and the
cottage's thick stone walls shielded you from the weather that
whined day after day to get in. The aim: to create a little bauble
of serenity far away from that niggle of anxiety that now
followed you in the city wherever you went. Because it wasn't

16

safe for your type to go to cinemas or public pools any more, to markets and shopping malls, anywhere that people would congregate. Then petrol stations became a worry. Theatres. Airports. And far, far away from all that Motl and you were determined to make your world like a furnace lit, a furnace of warmth and light. Fat lovely life of love, in your little glow home, and how fiercely you cherished it. The pleasing circularity of your life. You were reclaiming childhood here, and simplicity; shedding the city crust.

Free yourself of ties as a fish breaks through a net.

∽ 10 ∾

The three of them spin, talking through the bewilderment.

'Look. The bed's wider than it's long . . .'

'. . . which only happens when you're rich.'

'The coat hangers in the cupboard are really stubborn . . .'

'. . . they won't come off.'

'The shower head's as big as a dinner plate . . .'

'You know, I don't think Mum and Dad have anything to do with this. It's all too . . . *careful*.'

'They're not here. Anywhere. They're not. I know it.'

At Mouse's bitter conclusion, absolute quiet. Because they're utterly alone. And the realisation is like stepping from the warmth of a fire-toasty house into the formal cold of a deep winter night. Tidge paces the room. Brushes the walls. Recoils. Too cold, too soundproofed. Mouse slides down the door, his hands cupped in horror at his mouth. Your worrier, always thinking too much. His anxiety's demanding like a toddler fresh from sleep.

'The window!' Tidge exclaims suddenly. They scramble.

A street. An old office building across the road. The eyes of its empty windows as blank as the freshly dead. Everything abandoned, everything quiet. Traffic lights changing but no traffic anywhere, not a car, not a bike. Endlessly and obediently the traffic lights changing but no people anywhere. No life.

'It feels like the proper world has stopped,' Tidge says quietly, in wonder, pressing into thick glass that doesn't bend.

'Like we're the last ones left,' his twin brother whispers.

Soli shivers like a pony. As do you.

> *For the world has lost its youth,*
> *and the times begin to wax old.*

❦ 11 ❧

Motl and you battened down the hatches on your country's strife. Created your little bauble of enchantment far away from everything while you sat the new politics out. And the new life was good, varnished with love and light. Motl was the teacher. He was born to it, he should have done it from the start. He'd grab the kids by the shoulders and tell them to go to the window and look, *look*, you wallies, because there was never nothing there. 'A cloud like a rocking horse!' 'A one-legged seagull!' 'A snail's frilled foot!' 'Look at the sea inhaling and exhaling but it's the tide and it's governed by the moon.' 'Look at the stained-glass window of that grasshopper's wing, that's your art lesson.' 'Biology, the carpet beetle's defensive curl.' '*Don't* ask me one more time, What are we doing next? Work it out for yourself! Explore everything, debate, rip the world apart. I want *thinkers*. Children who question everything. Who have vigorous, audacious, independent thought!' And eventually, they forgot to ask, What are we doing next?

Taking it in turns to dance with their cheeks to his belt buckle and their feet on the pedals of his shoes as you'd sing your favourite song line, 'I will wrap you in kisses', and demonstrate. And everyone rushing outside when dolphins leapt past and standing in a row and whooping at the lovely oblivious joy of them, and at night Motl and you lifting each child solemnly to the high canopy of stars and telling them not to worry because you're all in the magic house now, it will look after you, you're safe here, you're safe.

And now, and now, you wear them like a coat. Their squirmy demanding heat. That can never be taken from you. You envy the air in the room they're in, rubbing up close. The silence here is a presence, constantly watching, listening, taking note. You need to be released into the outrageously beautiful world. Can't. Bear. This.

*The sun and all light have forever fused themselves
into my heart and upon my skin.*

⤬ 12 ⤬

Out of the window a ferocious sunset falls away. The colour of blood in it. Lightning spits and flickers in the distance as if it's a faulty fluorescent light. A tree right outside tosses its branches at the approaching storm like a horse spooked. 'No panicking, all right.' Soli. A tremor in her voice she can't iron out. She checks her new watch. So, obediently, do her little brothers. They all received them on your final night. They say 1707. The kids don't get it. What happened to the past day? They woke just after 4 p.m., on the bed, in a line, on their backs. They've never slept so late in their lives. And they're still tired but it's an unearthly tired as if some enormous rake is dragging them down and pulling them back into sleep.

They're fighting it. Tidge: shaking his arms like an actor warming up. Mouse: jogging fast on the spot. Soli: biting her lip because she's the eldest and is used to getting what she wants and no way is that sleep having her back. Because of the things that now happen in it. Because it can't be trusted. Because of the terror that could envelop them if unconsciousness, once again, gets its chance.

We have got ready the fire whose smoke will enwrap them:
and if they implore help,
helped shall they be with water like molten brass
which will scald their faces.

❧ 13 ❧

Motl and you wormed that fat little teapot of a house into all their hearts. You both dreaded a blunting when wonder would not cradle them but it never came, for the two of you pulled happiness around them like a wondrous cape. So much of it in this briny new life! You'd forgotten how to be a mother immersed in Project Indigo, but Salt Cottage taught you that a nanny makes you afraid of your kids and it's so much richer to do it all yourself. They chisel out your deepest feelings, your wildest love and rage and frustration and euphoria, they haul you to the coalface of life. You could be distant, remote without them; but as a parent you were forced to participate. And to your shock you revelled in it. These were the shining hours; the kids burnished your life.

There were complaints, of course. About the new poorness. Crockery chipping and not being replaced, duvets stuffed with newspaper, baths topped up with saucepans from the stove. Complaints about windows encrusted with salt because there wasn't a cleaning lady any more and about your cooking which you never did quite well enough ('Not cereal for dinner *again.*' 'My repertoire is extremely limited, all right? I'm a scientist, not a cook. Give me a Bunsen burner and you'd really see something bubble up.' Cue Motl, cowering under the table, 'No, no, anything but that!').

And gradually the whining stopped because each of you knew

that Salt Cottage meant one thing above anything else – *survival.*
You were safe here, you were safe. And it was enough.

> *He who is an alien to grace*
> *seeks and finds naught but disgrace and adversity:*
> *if thorny brambles grow, it is the requital of his sowing.*

⤴ 14 ⤵

'Hey, I remember something now.' Mouse presses his knuckles to his temples. 'It's coming . . . from last night . . .' He's screwing up his eyes as if trying to squeeze memory out. You lean.

'Okay. I was lying in my bed. Trying to fall to sleep. Then Dad came in. He lay down next to me and put his hand over my mouth. There was a hanky on it. He was whispering, "Sssh, little man, sssh," but his voice was full . . . like, like there was crying in it. And I was breathing in but feeling funny and then Dad was holding me and clamping me tight and then he was sealing off my talking and then, and then, this is the really scary bit, it was like I was slipping into this sea of the inkiest, scariest black, like some body in a coffin being slid from a ship and then the dark was crowding over me and just before I was completely under Dad was curling around me and clinging on, tight, like I was some life buoy in this vast ocean of fear . . .' Your little boy looks straight at his brother and sister. Frightened eyes. A blink. 'Then no dreams. Nothing. Just this enormous blank . . .'

'Like being dead.' Tidge, quiet.

The brothers look at each other. Pins and needles take over their eyes. They're both blinking like two ships sending out distress signals and the crying's coming now, a great dumping wave of it; young, so young, too young for this.

Verily every soul has as a surety a guardian over it.

∽ 15 ∽

On a clear still night your neighbour, Ulla Ween, came around. A man of the book, flinty and devout. His house was a mile away. He was the only neighbour close. It was a Monday. He often popped in on a Monday for a meal; he lived by himself. He'd supervised your building work with heavy eyelids and weirdly bobbed hair and lips always wet. On this particular Monday Ulla Ween sat at your kitchen table and ate a meal as he always did then licked his plate clean which he never did, and placed it carefully down. He said you'd soon be informed that Salt Cottage belonged to someone else. With a peculiar smile on his face. Like he was trying to hold in the delight. You snorted a laugh. Motl stood. Because in an instant your neighbour had become someone else. He told you that it was a correcting of past iniquities. 'Pardon?' You laughed again, unsure, your face not getting the joke. Without another word he tucked the dinner plate under his arm and walked out, that peculiar smile still on his face. You stood in shock. Threw your own plate after him with more physical fury than you'd ever shown in your life. The china smashed and gravy dribbled down. You had finally got the joke.

'*That* is a man completely untroubled by compassion,' you declared as you wiped your hands of him smartly on your hips.

And from that evening onward the future darkened around you, you could all feel it contract. History was close on that night; the world was pushing against the windows, beating the glass with its hungry palms; wanting in. And in the early hours you slipped into Mouse's bottom-bunk bed and curled your arm over him and burrowed into his lovely warmth. You need to do that whenever the thinking flurries in your head too much, when you can't hook on to sleep no matter how hard you try and there's only one thing guaranteed to work: your children. Only they can distract you enough, balm you down into it.

Now now now. Strapped to the guilt of what you did once.

The small man builds cages for everyone he knows.

∞ 16 ∞

'You know, nothing looks like it's going to hurt us.' Soli assesses the creamy serenity of their room. 'It looks, actually, kind of . . . posh. Eh?'

'Mum?' Mouse asks the quiet. 'Dad?'

Silence, as vast as a desert.

His sister gnaws at a sliver of skin on her finger. There's blood; she pops it in her mouth. Fingers the doorknob, worrying about so much, you can tell: the rattling that'll be back with the consistency of a playground bully and she's meant to be the mother here and how will she get the boys through the night? Hardwired into her is caring, giving, pleasing, the female lot; as a baby she'd offer the milk bottle back to you, place it insistently in your mouth. The boys never did that. Womanhood is a condition of giving, continually, and it astounds you how early it manifests itself.

'Maybe the rattler has left for the evening,' she says brightly. 'For twelve hours. At least. Until daytime.' But her voice grows wobblier as she speaks.

Mouse hrumphs away. Scrunches his hands under his armpits. Feels his pyjama pocket. Finds Motl's old silver pen with his name in a flourish along it. Your husband had slipped it to him as he curled around him on the final night because he knows that writing will give him solace, will firm him up. A smile opens his face. The pen he's not meant to touch! That makes his writing come out neat! 'Guys, *look*.' He holds it high, along with a tiny notebook. 'They were in my pocket! So

28

perhaps . . . there's a plan here.' Tidge flops onto the bed with relief. Mouse lies belly-down on the floor and feverishly writes. 'Tell our story, tell the truth,' you'd whispered to your little scribe as he was deeply caught by unnatural sleep. Tell our story because erasure is what this new government is so effective at now and children have to be just as slippery as adults, they have to be wily, to think. Like grown-ups.

WE WILL GET OUT!!!!

His words shout with all the certainty of childhood.

Tidge leaps up, glee in his eyes. Tugs at the curtains. Yep, they'll hold, they'll do for a Tarzan rope. 'Come on, guys!' he rallies.

You laugh. God help this careful room. Motl and you haven't dubbed them the Ferals for nothing. Your three vivid-hearted kids, so brimming with life. The rapture of them, the rapture; you feel haloed by light as you watch.

And now back to your own words. To stoke up your own fire, to nurture the blaze, the warmth. Back to all your husband's books and his scribbles crowded irreverently into every sacred volume, into margins and the front of them and the back. Quotes, arguments, provocations, thoughts. Once, long ago, it was compilation cassettes; now this. What did he tell you near the end? You were barely listening, you'd tuned out. 'Ageing has become this process of retreating from certainty, but not in a terrifying way, a wondrous way. *Listen*, you. In mystery lies the sublime, that's the only way I can describe it, and it's a shocking, transforming journey and I'm absolutely loving it. I can finally be myself. The *relief* of it, lovely. The relief.' He'd gone on some momentous journey, and you had little idea of it, had zoned out.

*When I am painting I feel happy
and I let the feeling take hold of my hand.*

∞ 17 ∞

A letter arrived the day after your neighbour's visit. A scrawl. No name attached. Someone helping out. You'd been tracked down. Would be recalled to Project Indigo. You were the missing piece of the jigsaw and it could proceed no further without you. And they were close, so close to completion. The letter urged you to think carefully of the consequences. To consider fleeing Salt Cottage. Disappearing, fast, to somewhere you'd never be found out.

'*Who* let on we were here?' You scrunched up the paper and flung it into the bin.

'Maybe it wasn't too hard to work out,' Motl said quietly.

He retrieved the letter and smoothed it down with his fingertips. A bell jar of quiet fell over him. The rest of you gathered at the kitchen table, hushed. He smoothed down that letter long after he'd finished reading, smoothed and smoothed it, couldn't stop. You knew his thinking. He'd seen it all coming. He was always going to get his family away, make you one hundred per cent safe, have you emigrate. To become refugees like his sister, the professor who one day had had enough of the raids on her history department and the falling student numbers because the new slogan was *The More You Read The More Stupid You Become*, so what, any more, was the point. The Great Leap Back, that's what she dubbed it as she explained why she was pulling out. Her brother's family was to follow. Next summer, winter, year. Ah yes. Your pottering, dreamy, boy of a man. Always so good at procrastinating and sleeping in and handing his papers in late. Brilliant, yes, but. Then one day 'getting out' was too late – the borders were closed off. You were trapped.

And not one of you around that kitchen table said a word as Motl smoothed that letter down, smoothed it and smoothed it until it ripped. The letter shrilling at you to abandon the magic house.

We are made a spectacle unto the world, and to angels.

∾ 18 ∾

Night unfurls. A pow–wow abruptly halts. Fury hangs in the air. Soli keeps saying, 'It's going to be all right,' in a silky mother tone but it doesn't come out right, it just winds her little brothers up. Who gave her permission to be so knowing in this place?

'Mummy-stealer!' Tidge shouts. 'Stop using that voice.'

'It's going to be all right.'

'But the doorknob?' Mouse fires at her, rat tat tat. 'And this room? And the kick?' He's the expert at questions and you're always encouraging it except when a migraine's coming and then he has to stop. 'Everything is *so* not okay,' he flings. 'I saw your face when that key came. You had no idea what it means and no idea what's next. There was this flinch, in your eye, it *told* me. It was like a music counter going tic tic tic.'

'Everything will be okay,' she soothes again.

Mouse storms off to the room's cupboard and curls inside, his notebook a teddy to his chest. His brother props his elbows at the window and stares out. Your girl is abandoned. She's failed and she so rarely does that, she's your high achiever who likes everything to be just right. She curls on her side on the bed. The flinch in her eye going tic tic tic.

However irritated you may feel, never speak harshly.

❧ 19 ❧

Eventually Soli unwraps her limbs and coaxes Tidge back to her. Finally he comes. She lies with him, her arm a seatbelt over his torso. She holds and holds until he's soothed into the release of sleep, then gingerly extracts herself and pads to the cupboard.

'Come on, you. It's late.'

Mouse glares. Owl-awake. 'I'm keeping guard. Someone has to. Thank God you've got me in this place. A bit of gratefulness wouldn't go astray. Like, thanks, Mouse, for watching over us.'

No way is he getting back into that bed. You know why. There's no grown-up to insist and it's a room he doesn't trust, ditto a sister with a secret and a brother too accepting, who's fallen too easily into sleep. The moon outside is a sliver of a thumbnail. As bright as a bone. He's staying up with it, all night if he must. It's in the set of his mouth. Your worrier. Always thinking too much, everything cutting so deep. Too glary in his head is the enormity of navigating his way through life, he finds it so hard to shut off the fear. You're anxious about the teenager he'll become with all that complicated energy bottled up.

Your entire life, as a mother, is about anticipation. Of accidents, trip-ups, abductions, disasters. Second-guessing that walk to the corner shop, the crossing of the road, the swim at the beach, and God help them if they ever get near a motorbike.

You'll never stop the hovering. Motl says you have to, you must learn to let go. You retort that he doesn't worry enough.

> *I alone dare not seek rest.*
> *The ordinances of heaven are inexplicable*
> *but I will not dare to follow my friends and leave my post.*

⚮ 20 ⚯

Tidge is vastly asleep, dangling a leg off the bed and taunting his brother with his effortless flop. Soli told him to trust and that's exactly what he's doing. He's always the one who falls instantly into sleep. Motl says it's the mark of a contented soul.

Mouse writes with a staccato pen.

Look at him. God. Typical! SUCH a believer. NEVER thinking ENOUGH.

Unlike him. And you. All the thinking haranguing you awake, night after night.

Soli's now curled tight and troubled in unsmooth sleep. That strange-tired finally won. You long to brush the hair from her forehead and unfold all her folded bits, long to stretch her beautiful limbs back into lightness. No child should ever sleep so . . . condensed. Her eyes suddenly shine like marbles in the dark, she's awake. She looks around, trying to work out where she is. Sees Mouse. Remembers.

'I need a cuddle,' he says, quick, even though he's still annoyed at that mother voice she stole. But you know him. A magnet of need is pulling him into skin and warmth, any he can get. She'll do. They hold, and hold, in this unknown dark.

So small, alone, lost.

The cuddle works, stills them both. Because even though she's all angles and elbows and coltish length she gives the most enveloping hugs. Like you're a hot-water bottle warming her right through and she doesn't want to let go, ever. She's all-calming when she holds you and you've never told her the gift of it. So much you've never said. That you marvel at Mouse's mind, the cogs of it, the singularity of his thought. And Tidge's robust sunniness, his ability to weather turbulence. And the joy from all of them that floods you; that you feel stronger as a mother than you ever have in your life.

He who is unaffected by transiency can be called tranquil.

⊱ 21 ⊰

The soldiers came the afternoon the letter arrived. An aching bright day of air so scrubbed it hurt. There was so little time. Behind mirrored sunglasses you couldn't read their faces. Not even Tidge could fillet something from them and he's the heart-lifter of the family and his smile usually works. But these men didn't seem properly human any more, with proper hearts; their faces were set. They went straight to the study with Motl and you. The kids sat on the sofa. Found hands when the quiet became too much. Your husband asked you to leave at one point. You joined the children and quietly found two palms. Only your trembling spoke. You had just been told the other members of your research team had disappeared. '*Been* disappeared, or vanished?' you'd foolishly joked, in shock. No response. You were the only scientist left, that's all you knew; you, alone, could activate it.

The door finally opened and the soldiers walked out. Their sunglasses were gone.

'What's happening?' the kids asked. 'What's going on?'

The soldiers said nothing. They left. You rushed back to Motl. Finally came out with your arms around each other and you never do that.

'You both look smaller,' Tidge said, stepping back, 'like you've been shrunk.'

'What's going on?' Soli asked with a new maturity, a brother in each hand.

Your knuckles were little snow-capped mountains as you gripped your husband tight. Dread in your stomach like sickness. What to tell them? Yes, you were being recalled. A matter of national urgency. And the kids, the kids were to be 'relocated' whatever that meant. What not to tell them? That you knew these people in command. Men who had lost their light hearts. Knew the cruellest thing they could do to a woman, to get her to talk, was to hurt the children in some way and have the mother witness it. The shredded state of your country now felt like an offence against the natural order of things and by God you would not give these people the chance, you would not.

And then the extraordinary part, and you can still scarcely believe it. Motl had wheedled one last night at home. Alone, with just the family. Because he had once tutored the soldier-in-command and had made him laugh and had given him an extension on his final paper when his mother was dying of cancer and had even written a condolence note and it was all remembered, that. His gentleness was trusted. He's that kind of person. He shines goodness and people are drawn to it.

But so little time. A night, one night to reconfigure your life. What to tell the kids? What not? That their wind-licked little house would now be someone else's. A start, yes, they would have to face it, this was how your country now worked. 'Pardon?' Mouse yelled in disbelief. An enormous rage at the unfairness of it all took over him and he slid down a wall, and became a howl. Roared great choking sobs. As abandoned as a toddler in a crowd.

'This is the magic house. We're safe here, we're safe. You said.'

You looked wildly around at your family and put your hands over your ears and ran outside, couldn't bear it any more, the news or the noise, ran down to the beach, to the kelp-heavy waves heaving their load, to a gull that didn't move on the sand as the water rushed hungrily around its legs and didn't move as you stood there breathing deep, didn't move as you sucked in the sharpness of the air as if you were filling up your body. This land was your cathedral. Its yowling hurting ringing light. It held your heart hostage; you dreamed of being slipped into its soil like a sacrament upon death. And now you were being ripped from it. And every one of your little family. Because of your past catching up.

God's beauty has split me wide open.

❧ 22 ❧

Behind you on that beach, Motl's voice. 'Stay back, leave her alone.' You turned just in time to catch Soli – a flinty ball of fury – punching her father hard in the stomach. Ramming into him all her rage at his hesitation and mildness, all her rage at the teasing little boy inside him that sometimes riles you both so much.

'Who *says* to leave her alone? If it wasn't for you we'd be out of this country by now. You were going to do it but you never got around to it. If it wasn't for you we'd be *safe*.'

He didn't say, no, actually, it was your mother who got us into this. Have you ever loved him so fiercely? But suddenly, an old man. Without any words. Who did only this.

He bent down. Held Soli tight. Clamped her furious churn in his arms and stilled it and stilled it until all the sobbing was gone and she went limp.

Where is he now? Your good, gentle man who you never valued enough. You shut your eyes at the memory of him pushing into your skin. Resolve melting like water thrown over ice in a sink. Opening out like a flower as he unlocked you into life. Your want is unsinkable, undrownable; like a bottle corked it will travel the world searching for him, for shelter and shore, for vast rest. The man who brewed happiness into your life. When a marriage works there's nothing more soldering and you were given the gift of it. You were so different yet it worked; if you didn't have him there'd be no one else you'd want. He'd endured so much throughout the years, been battered again and again, but you know now that there are people who teach with their quiet grace. How to endure. By their courage and evenness. They help us to find our own strength.

And now you are alone.

Love is composed of a single soul inhabiting two bodies.

❦ 23 ❦

Mouse writes to stay awake deep into this vulnerable night.

1. *Door. QUIET LIKE SOME TOMB when I press my ear into it. Why? Soundproofed?*
2. *Walls. THICK AND COLD. Okay. Like they're collecting all the chill of all the nights into them and holding it in tight like the cold in some COFFIN down deep in the ground.*
3. *Bathroom. Hmm. FRESHLY PAINTED. Who was here before us? What went on?*

Thinking too much. Because the room they're in is a basement and basements are where things happen. They're not used to half-below-ground level. They live up close to a huge clean sky, a big dramatic one, under the thumb of the weather. The sun in their bones. Your daughter's had a dream, for years now, of being trapped under the earth; of hearing close above her a child's thudding running and a distant bird and squeaky needles of grass being pulled up and the deep breathing of someone who's flopped belly down and is soaking up the warm lovely sunshine, completely oblivious to her underneath, scrambling and panicking and unable to get out. It never fails to whoosh her into waking with a pounding heart.

4. *Window. Glass that's NEVER going to break.*

They tried. The three of them tested it with a chair after the rattling doorknob came but it wouldn't smash, bend, give one bit.

The kind of glass you can see out of but not into. CREEPY.

Two layers of it with dead flies in between. Their feet twined like ballerinas.

Who was here before us? Did they get out? HOW?

Your lair of lost children under the earth. And all you can do is watch.

Hope deferred maketh the heart sick.

∽ 24 ∽

Motl became someone else after the soldiers left. He appeared in the kitchen with pyjamas poking from trouser legs and his old green sneakers without socks. He spray-painted I BET YOU MISS above the basketball hoop on the garage. He strode around the house with a book by Kafka like a vicar with a Bible clutched at his chest. He chopped onions while wearing swimming goggles and muttered under his breath.

'Don't worry,' you said breezily to the kids, 'Dad's just sorting things out.'

'Yay!' the boys squealed. Because to them, he's the champion at that. The chief surgeon at the toy hospital where patients are checked in overnight and by morning limbs are secured and remote controls have sprung into life.

But as you watched those onions being methodically attacked you couldn't help throw across, 'I prefer to cry, mate.'

'Be quiet, be quiet, I'm *thinking*,' your husband exploded.

You all went quiet. For the depth of Motl's anger was shocking. You'd never seen it before and you thought you knew him so well. Thought, suddenly, my God, who is this man? You didn't recognise him at all, he was someone new.

A person who the world had caught out, yes. A man whose finely crafted code of goodness, that had spined his whole life, had been overturned in the blink of an eye. He used to say that a gentleman always does the kind thing but that didn't work any more. He was one of those old-fashioned sorts of people

44

who was caring and polite and thought it was the proper way to exist. Mouse asked him once, as a toddler, 'Daddy, are you from the past?' He was the man who never told his parents he knew the tooth fairy wasn't real because he didn't want to hurt their feelings, who fed sparrows in his garden until they were too fat to fly, who opened doors and stood on buses and wrote thank you notes. You married him for all that. He attracted extreme people like a magnet because of his core of stability and quiet. But those types of men now seemed soft and naïve and weak. In this new, sour-spirited world, people like Motl were swallowed up. And he knew it.

> *Ask your heart to decide;*
> *righteousness is what the soul and the heart*
> *feel tranquil about;*
> *and sinfulness is what is fixed in the soul,*
> *and roams about in the breast.*

❦ 25 ❧

Mouse makes another expedition and another back to his sleeping brother and sister. He slips his arm over them both and burrows close. A skin diver, diving in, cupping his brother's serenely heaving chest and breathing in his slumbering deep, deep, wanting some of that trust to rub off. Tidge's crossed his fingers and Mouse unlocks them and they wait for a beat then spring back. Mouse chuckles. His would never do that, you'd need pliers to pull them apart.

Hey. Mum talked to us about pale rooms like this. Once.

You did, yes. Creamy rooms from your college days. After you'd drunk a bottle of champagne Motl had smuggled home because he knew it would soar your heart and perhaps, with luck, turn you into the woman he remembered once. He burst through the door holding high his prize and you smiled with your eyes just slits like a cat with the warmest sill of sun. Then you summonsed them all to your high wide bed and were transformed into someone else. Young again, light, loose. And Motl was all cackly with glee as he handed across your last, cherished, bone china teacup, the one with the red spots, but it was full of champagne.

Then the stories came. Of university days when your country was something else. Of houses with roaring fires whose heat made your face go tight. Of windows three storeys high looking

46

over oceans of green. Of carpets so soft you could sleep on them. And you did, long ago, at parties that began at midnight and lasted until dawn where you'd dance barefoot and dance until the softness of the floor pulled you down. And you'd wake beside people who were astonished to learn there were two ten o'clocks in the day, who never knew the meaning of grubbily grey clothes that had been white once or of plates crazed with cracks. Because those kinds of people lived lives of a delicate shade of cream. Which is exactly this waiting place.

But no, not exactly.

Because back then there was always a way out. A spider of fear picks its way up your spine. Those were days before Project Indigo, before all Motl's wariness over the direction it was heading in and where it was dragging your family let alone yourself.

'I'm just not comfortable with what you're doing any more. Religion gives you a framework to work in, and you scientists are creating this new priestly caste which seems every bit as arrogant and condescending as the old lot. Eh?' He poked you in the stomach for affirmation. 'I'm just not sure that humans are capable of a morality outside religion. Who, madam, is fencing you in? Anyone?'

'So you've found God, my love, after decades of intelligent rationalism?'

'Look, as a scientist, I've come across no evidence of a God existing. But I haven't come across any evidence of he or she *not* existing, and I'm intrigued by that. We have to understand that there are things in this world we cannot understand.'

You snorted your disgust.

Motl laughed. 'You lefty liberals are the most narrow-minded of the lot. So judgemental and indignant, bursting with all your pompous, righteous certainty. Extremely vulnerable, Missy, to your sheep-like opinions, don't you think? Urgh. All rattly and hollow and . . . un-calm . . . yes.'

47

'You believe in superstition, mate, I believe in fact.'

'I just can't quite believe that order came out of chaos, that's all.' He shrugged. 'The idea that God has created human beings makes more sense to me than he hasn't. Science isn't the only way to truth, my love. It can't actually explain how our world came into being. All the extraordinary complexity of it.'

'So you've found religion.'

'Not *quite*. Let's just say I'm surrendering to the mystery. There's a lot of solace I'm finding in my books. And I'm loving the journey, Mrs,' and he padded off to his study, full of chuff.

> *Let your diet be spare, your wants moderate,*
> *your needs few.*
> *So, living modestly, with no distracting desires,*
> *you will find content.*

❧ 26 ❧

A thud. Outside their door. Mouse gasps. Eyes wide, rabbit-still. Until he was five he'd pad into your room when the terrors of night became too much. You'd open out the duvet and sling him in close and he'd nestle against you like a door jamb to a door and you'd smile at the hot firm wedge of him and wish it would go on forever and want it now, so much. Everything's worse after dark when the fear crowds in. Those strange bumps and scrapes outside their door are like secrets being shifted in the dead of night and your boy is rigid with fear.

You long for rest. That moment of grace every night in Salt Cottage when you'd tiptoe into their bedroom and the short, sharp shock would come; alone, every night, standing in that room that was filled with the sleep of your children. Just ... breathing them in. Then a great warmth would flood through you, an enormous, glittery, heart-swelling gratitude, and you'd find yourself closing your eyes in unstoppable thanks. Prayer is gratitude, oh yes. You never told Motl of those luminous moments, can't understand what combusted within him, resolutely do not believe yet want to, need to, at times. Religion may be a delusion but it's a delusion of solace and there's something to be said for that. Yes, it may be all lies and creaky myth but what is this stillness that steals through you in moments, what? The short, sharp shock of it.

> *There is no need for temples; no need for*
> *complicated philosophy.*
> *Our own brain, our own heart is our temple.*

⊃ 27 ⊂

You drove that last afternoon at Salt Cottage. The five of you. Not too far because there would be roadblocks up ahead and none of you was completely convinced about that former student's heart. But far enough. A brisk breeze buffeted the car like a boat in a wind-tossed sea and you said to Motl to stop, you were going to be sick, and stumbled out and straightened and stood there tall with the stiff wind skating off the plain but flinch you would not, break you would not. Breathing in the spite of it but not bending, not giving an inch, tears streaming down your cheeks. That was the core of you then, holding your face to that sting and that hurt. Fury had become your glowing nub. The embers were intense and they would never soften out.

You drove home in silence. Held your cheeks high to the slit of the car window like a dog needing air. Your jeans were wet from the long grass and petals were crushed on your boots and dirt flecked your face; it was as if the land itself was trying to cling on to you, to hold you back. And you knew now what it was to be sick in your heart.

You will fight this dispossession and God willing your children's children will fight it if they must. Your land holds your heart hostage. You long to bury yourself in it, to stretch belly down and feel its warm soil in your blood and your bones, to prostrate yourself in its earth.

Not in the sky, not in the middle of an ocean,
not in a mountain cave,
can a man escape the effects of his ill deeds.

∞ 28 ∞

Maybe they cracked? Yeah. Maybe they ordered this because we WENT TOO FAR. So, like, we've been cast out and this is our punishment and they're above us in the roof – he looks up – *surveilling everything and seeing how we cope.*

They were really pushing it towards the end. Among all the snipping and shouting between Motl and you were three kids flurried up. It was like flint in the air before a storm. Everything charged, as if each one had new batteries in. All the squabbling and Chinese-burning, the hair-pulling, name-calling, toy-snatching, kicking, biting, even that.

Then after that last drive, the stopping. Back in the house. That awful moment when the air itself seemed shocked. You, of course, at the centre of it. Becoming a woman you hadn't seen for years, since the kids were babies and they'd drag you into that deep, deep tired and you'd wake up tired and never find a firm footing with the day. Standing there wailing that you couldn't cope any more, couldn't cope, with your fingers curled frozen at your head and the bones in your hands little rakes. 'I can't do it any more,' you keened, 'can't – do – it.' All of it, everything. Motherhood, Motl, Project Indigo, the way it was vining your life, dragging everything along with it, all the uncertainty of what was coming next.

Then Tidge rushed in and clung like a wet plastic bag slicked about a tree, one that's impossible to prise off, and as you held

53

him tight you found calm again and apologised for the mother you'd become, and wept. They all ended up on you, trying to still you down but the shuddering wouldn't go, wouldn't stop.

Nup nup nup. Something else was breaking Mum that day, something far beyond any of us lot. Being here isn't because of plain old naughtiness. It's something FAR BIGGER than that. Is this all Mum's fault? Where is she? When is she coming?

I am as if intoxicated with the grief of my heart.

❧ 29 ❧

The final night at Salt Cottage. Rain-whipped. Sky pressing into the land, pummelling it; wet hammering the windows like a giant flinging pebbles; as if heaven itself was stopping anyone listening in. Your kitchen had the glow of a special occasion. Candles were lit. You were wearing your favourite perfume, the gardenia one, and Motl nursed a mug of his beloved whisky, the Ardbeg you love breathing in.

He had informed you earlier he had a plan. Fevery, excited, flushed. 'It will work.' You had to trust him. Why? Because those three children filled every inch of his heart as hugely as your own. He couldn't tell you exactly what the idea was. He said he was protecting them, and you. 'There are ways of extracting information, any information they want, you know that. It's too risky, Mum. For all of us.' And did you have a counter-plan? No, you did not.

Motl's fingers now drummed the kitchen table and when the whole family was settled he leaned close. You sucked in your lower lip: something in him had firmed and you loved him like this. He was one of those people whose mind is concentrated, magnificently, under pressure, who grow in stature once they've moved beyond the initial shock. He announced calmly that you would all be going away. Held up splayed hands to the questions. He said everyone had to remember two things and two only: that no situation had ever been improved by thinking it couldn't be changed, and you all had to keep on hoping even when hope seemed lost.

'What's happening?' 'Where are we going?' 'Can we have chocolate?' 'What's going on?'

Motl shook his head at the shrill of voices. He smiled. He said there was just one thing each child had to remember, to get them through, and they all had to listen carefully. He turned to his youngest. 'You, my little book muncher of the family, have to write everything down. Be our memoriser. Tell our story, tell the truth.'

Mouse nodded, thrilled with the weight of his task.

The professor turned to his daughter. 'You, madam, my big, beautiful girl, have to look after your brothers. Be the mummy of the group.'

Even now you can hear Soli's deep, wavery breathing as she contemplated the enormity of that.

Then his older son. 'And you, my sunny soldier boy, have to believe. Keep up the hope and keep smiling, for all of us. Be buoyant. That's all. Set an example for your brother and sister.' Motl has told you that he thinks Tidge is one of those people who can plug themselves into light and be an enormous light to others. 'Belief will be your shelter, all right?'

'Eh?' His boy yelped in bewilderment but Motl didn't have time to explain any further; he asked everyone to hold hands and with an enormous impish glee declared he had a secret, the most secret of secrets, and as he spoke the hairs stood shrill to attention on the back of your neck.

'One day we'll come back to Salt Cottage. I *promise*. I have a plan.'

But he wouldn't say what. And you remember clearly the shine in his face as he spoke because it reminded you of nothing so much as some lone, crazy, heart-bursting salmon, fighting its way up river, never stopping until it's home. Then Motl tented his fingers under his chin and declared that this new regime would eventually collapse because it was a denial of every single human value that was good and civilised and right. Because it shrivelled people's hearts to just two emotions: fear, and a desperate, ugly sense of self-preservation. Because it stopped friends and neighbours trusting each other. Because it killed history by rewriting the books. And lastly, obscenely, because it stole joy. Anyone's right.

'And all this is being done in the name of freedom,' you spat, in a voice they'd never heard.

The whole family looked across. Because you had become old, it had begun from that night. But Motl was all-calming. He murmured 'Mum' in his warning voice. He said people can choose to live as victims or courageous fighters and we all had to think very carefully about how we proceeded from this point. And that there are some people who are broken by unfairness, and there are some people who are not.

'And we will not be. We will not.'

> *Old is my body, heavy and frail,*
> *it moves not with my fleeter thoughts.*
> *But strong my purpose, strong my heart.*

❧ 30 ❧

Mouse's eyes aren't working properly any more. He's rubbing them, they're filmy, scratchy, raw. His writing has grown ragged, the notebook drops. He's curled at the foot of the bed; surrendering, finally, to sleep. On the floor, just like he used to approaching six, when he couldn't bear to hear his father's hrumph of annoyance any more but was still terrified of the dark so he'd pad into your room and lie meekly on the carpet so as not to wake you both up. In the morning the politeness of his curled little body on the hard floor would break your heart; you couldn't, possibly, get cross. Children are so much better than adults.

Tidge's the big brother only just. Mouse got stuck and had to be dragged out, Tidge just . . . slid. That about sums them up. The first boy was baked to perfection but the second emerged a touch overcooked, his skin raw and angry with rash. And upon arrival your youngest child took one look at his big brother and yowled a howl that sliced through the room. It was as if he sensed right then that this beautiful creature would dog him his entire life, that his big brother had glamour and he did not. For the elder is like one of those mysterious creatures from the ocean depths who glow, unstoppably, with an inner light. And Tidge's taller. You don't know what happened to Mouse's inches, they just got lost in the unfairness of the genetic lottery. 'Tidge'll never get spots as a teenager,' he wailed to you once, and you fear he's right. Your youngest is a head-downer as he talks, he's not used to the slap of face-to-face. He has a gift for aloneness and moodiness and withdrawal, from birth that pattern was set.

They arrived early. Your waters broke at thirty-two weeks and they were rushed into incubators and prodded and pierced with all manner of equipment slipped under pale, translucent flesh while you turned, couldn't bear it, and wept. And late that night, their first night in the hospital, Motl sensed Mouse's retreat from this world: after twelve hours he'd had enough. 'Don't go,' he pleaded to his fragile bundle of flesh, 'hold on, little man, it really can be wonderful in this place.' But his pleas weren't enough, they didn't convince. Then with flurrying fingers Motl listened to his heart and did something he absolutely wasn't cleared to do: he unplugged the little scrap of life not much bigger than his hand. He lifted it clear of his plastic box. He placed it next to his big brother.

Tidge pressed close. He curled his tiny fingers into his brother's flesh. Squeezed. Hauled him into this life.

Mouse's got a lot to be grateful for. You're always saying it in your warning voice. Which your daughter often repeats. Soli, Soli, Soli. Your prickly slip of a girl who's always trying so hard to be good, to get everything right. Will you grow old in terror of each other, as mother and daughter, of the hurt you can both inflict? Please no. The professor and you did all your experimenting with her, the first-born; you were working the whole parent thing out. You both hovered so much, loving so fiercely, sneaking into her room and standing by her cot and just gazing, in awe, night after night. So much relaxing to get right, letting-go to learn, so much fear at the outset. Of all those things you were told children snatch from you: money, control, self-esteem, beauty, youth. It took a long time to learn what they inject: confidence, gratitude, strength.

And now, speeding into womanhood. You've always been *enchanted* by her. Always glancing at her effortless loveliness.

As for Motl, he looks at her in a way you've never seen before, like he looks at no one else in his life. Certainly not his wife. Some women are jealous of the gaze that fathers reserve for their daughters, but with Motl it makes you laugh. It's so . . . naked. Adoring, reverent, astounded, chuffed. Evangeline was the nickname she chose for herself for when she's a pop star when she's grown up. 'It's entirely inappropriate,' Motl's always teasing her, but you're not so sure. She's better than you. The wonder of that.

O thou enwrapped.

∽ 31 ∽

After that dinner at Salt Cottage Motl and you handed out the watches the three of them now wear on their wrists. 'We'd been saving them for the summer hols,' you rasped, your voice filling up, 'but, hey, you might as well have them tonight.' Then you clamped each of them tight like you were trying to breathe in their skin, to imprint it onto your own so you'd always have it close; their particular smell, each one so different, that you've known their entire lives. Trying to soak them into your dress so that in the future you can hold it to your face and breathe them back.

Later that night Motl and you curled around each of them and put a hanky over their mouths and clung to their lovely trusting warmth like they were life buoys in a vast ocean of fear and neither of you knew when land would be reached. Then everything went black – *'like death, I guess'* – and the three of them woke in this other world entirely, this pale, waiting place. Cast adrift, your fragile boats, and you all hope for landfall so much.

You had assumed Motl had told them what was happening; you trusted him to lead them to safety; where *is* he in all of this? What happened? Is he all right?

Your memory, just before your own world went black: Motl and you waiting, holding hands, side by side in your armchairs in a quiet the cottage never has. The arc of a car light. 'They're here.' Your husband, quiet. A quick squeeze of your hand. They came in through the unlocked door; no knock. A blast of cold wind from outside blew through you to the embered place inside they cannot reach, they can never reach. You blazed life. As you sat there waiting with your eyes shut for whatever was ahead. Because it was the only way it could be done. To save the children, to free them, that's what Motl had told you; otherwise the family would be hunted down like injured animals and the pursuit would never stop, there would never be any rest, any peace. 'Trust me,' he said, 'I have a plan. It's only you they want.'

So. You were gently but firmly grabbed from behind. Pulled to your feet. Pinioned by your wrists which were then cuffed to a belt and a hood was placed over you, cutting off any light. Shortly afterwards, a sharp blow and your world went blank, everything addled, your family lost. And now you are here, in this place.

Mouse jerks awake.

Okay, okay. Something else. From that last night at Salt Cottage. Dad crying but trying not to. His tiny spasms held in. I've never seen him cry before. I WISH I HADN'T REMEMBERED THAT. I wish wish WISH we were all back there. Back. Please, get us back.

Now is the time when what you believe in is put to the test.

Set me as a seal upon thine heart.

❧ 32 ❧

You need to burst into their room right now. Need to climb into their dark world and flick on the light and spring-clean it with your laugh. Want their glee back. You know each of their giggles exactly, they're like three fingerprints of joy and you'll always hold them tight, so tight, in the fist of your heart.

'Trust me,' that's what he said, 'never forget that.' But it's so hard to hold on to.

> *This is the way to die:*
> *Beauty keeps laying its sharp knife against me.*

❧ 33 ❧

Early morning. Tidge still vastly under. His face smooth as if it's lit from within, his eyelids shiny like they've been brushed with Vaseline. Mouse awake. Rises stiff. The night's anxiety still curled in his bones and even more nagged by worry now. Because dawn's here, the closeness of a key that works. Light slits open the black. Brightness comes quickly and he runs to the window and presses his palms to the sky and wants to dive up, up into that wide happy blue, wants to lick the lovely air. Footsteps. Outside. In suits and heels as they brisk along in that hurried way that city feet do. Your boy knocks on the glass but they cannot see or hear; unknowing they pass. Cars, finally. Thank goodness. He picks up his notebook.

The traffic lights have a reason now. I was getting worried for them, they looked so forlorn. Like they'd been stood up.

The busyness of the waking city seeps into the room and your youngest stands sentinel, waiting for goodness knows what: Motl and you perhaps to rush into this place and scoop them up whooping and laughing with relief but then his eyes squeeze shut – no, no – he shakes his head, no more crying's allowed out, Dad wouldn't want it.

But they didn't come. They didn't get us out. We're ALONE.
What happens to grown-ups when their past catches up? And
their kids. NO FAIR what happens to them. NO FAIR.

<u>Your hand sits in the classroom of God.</u>

❦ 34 ❦

Hot water ticks in the old pipes. Groans. Shudders. The building's waking up. Mouse's fingertips push at the glass. People walk by unaware of the panic fermenting at their feet. He looks at the bed and hesitates; soon he'll have to wake his siblings but he can't quite do it yet. They need their sleep. The warm shock of his caring heart; one of those moments when you think, hey, what's the worry, he'll be all right. Your dear, dear boy, trying so hard to be the man for a bit. He smooths a lock of hair from his sister's face. She needs her sleep, the weight of responsibility is scowling her up; she's got a new line in her forehead from trying so hard to be the mother of the group. And he doesn't want to crash all his anxiety into his brother just yet. This will swamp him. That nothing has changed, that you never came in the night.

Well well.

His brother's woken like he's heard his thinking. Mouse burrows under the covers. 'They're not here, dude,' he says, 'and there were noises. Outside the door. And there'll be a key soon and . . . I'm scared. Tidgy? I want to go home.'

His brother gulps, eyes wide, trying to remember Motl's words, to hold on to hope. He opens his mouth, nothing comes out, terror clogging his talk. And so here they are now, your beautiful boys, waiting, minute by snail minute. For goodness knows what. Deep wavery breathing from them both. Now their boxers are back. Punch-*punch,* punch-*punch.* Jabbing away at their skin. As they stare out at the morning they can't get to. At the window they cannot break.

> *Watchman, what of the night?*
> *Watchman, what of the night?*
> *The watchman said the morning cometh,*
> *and also the night.*

❧ 35 ❧

This will not defeat you. Light is anyone's birthright and you want it back. By heart you know Salt Cottage. Those words are not accidental. By *heart*.

The winds blew and beat upon that house and it fell not: it was founded upon a rock.

36

A group is being hurried down the street. Mothers and grandmothers and children. The littlest are crying. The mothers are pulling them along with still, hollow faces like the life has been walloped from them. Even the smallest hold bags. Some are just plastic from the supermarket. Several have coats over their pyjamas as if they've been caught in their sleep.

'Where are the boys?' Tidge asks. There are small ones, yes, but none over seven or eight.

'I don't know, dude,' Mouse replies. And as he speaks it is like mercury coming into you, seeping through your veins, its stately chill. 'I don't know,' your youngest repeats, rubbing mist from the window, from the horrified O of his mouth.

'The boys are with their dads,' your daughter interjects, teacher-bright. 'They're on their way to school.'

But a glittery quiet. As the three of them keep watching. Mouse's tongue blunted now and you know why. Because he overheard Motl and you talking once about fields on the edge of the city with freshly turned soil that trembled for three days then stopped.

'Why, Mummy, why?'

'Sssh, darling, not now, get some sleep.'

But knowing snapped open in him like a switchblade.

EVERYTHING is too close.

Your wild love. Your wild love.

They make haste to shed innocent blood.

∞ 37 ∞

Busyness has come. The city's tootling on with its day. Sunlight bursts through gliding clouds and a big happy blue hollers for the three of them to get out. Outside the window a plastic bag turns cartwheels on the street, joy riding on the breeze. People hurry about in their too-busy-for-stopping way that city feet do. The doorknob spins and spins catching on nothing. They've all had a go and everything is too quiet in this pale cocoon of a room but not in a calm way, a birds-hushed-before-an-earth-quake way.

'I wonder what happened in this place. You know, before,' Tidge wonders aloud.

Mouse still can't talk. Thinking too much.

Our turn will come. And all we can do is stand here and stand here waiting for goodness knows what.

Because of what you did once.

Then said I, Lord, how long?

❧ 38 ❧

Okay. What I've heard because no one's telling me, are they?
Dad saying this regime stops people being human but Mum
saying it doesn't stop people being human it brings out the worst
in them, what lies buried in everyone underneath. That we all
have this animal inside us, every single human being, and Dad
says, no, Mrs, not everyone, and then it's a fight. Mum all shouty
that everyone has this capacity to be inventively, viciously cruel,
to any person who's the outsider — the threat — and it's been
like that since humankind began and it will never stop and then
the stories come and I crouch under the stairs winded by the
listening. What grown-ups do. New-born babies put outside a
mother's cell in a bag with a starving cat. Jumping on a back
until it breaks. Pigeons stuffed into mouths. Eyes gouged out
with spoons. Drilled flesh. Villages gassed. Families holding tight
in the centre of a room and single people at the edges by them-
selves. Parents forced to shoot their children as punishment.
Parents forced to watch as their children's throats are slit. Parents
forced to watch as their children are starved to death. Mothers
beaten by their babies until the babies are dead. Right. What
grown-ups do. All of this. MUM? DAD? Are you out there? CAN
YOU COME? Please come.

So. All those scraps of late-night conversation that he's caught
in Salt Cottage when he should be asleep but he's been listening
from his cupboard under the stairs and his scream is his pen

and you're being filleted as he writes, everything that is beating and warm within you because childhood, any childhood, is not meant to be this and how does it get to this point.

I beseech you, in the bowels of Christ,
think it possible you may be mistaken.

❧ 39 ❧

They're all awake. In a line, contemplating a television with legs in the corner. 'It means it's really, really old,' Tidge says solemnly. None of them can get it to work. Your TV junkie can't understand the cruelty of one blank. 'Maybe there's a hidden camera in it.' Tidge comes up close. 'Maybe the three of us are in some freaky experiment and Mum and Dad are watching, to see how we cope. You know, a reality TV kind of thing.' He flashes his smile that melts everyone but his family and holds a hand flat to his heart. 'I must stop saying I'm hungry all the time. I must be kind to my sister and brother. I must share all my chocolate. I must blow the TV kisses. A lot.' He gives it a big smooch.

'I don't think so,' Mouse says. He lies in front of the screen staring in. 'Maybe they're dead,' he says softly, and you shut your eyes and hover your love, in the vivid air; imagine lying along the length of their backs, pressing into them calm and strength.

'The dead help, Dad says so,' your daughter responds, in that strangely dispassionate way kids sometimes have when talking about death; as if so what.

'No!' Tidge cries. 'They are not, they are *not*. Maybe they're being tormented by us here. Imagine that? And there'll be no food ever and they'll be watching us as we turn on each other

and then get quieter and quieter, and close our eyes, and . . .
stop . . . finally. Maybe it's the way to get them to talk.'
Everyone quiet. Thinking of that.

And God will say, 'Taste ye your own doings.'

❧ 40 ❧

The doorknob. The rattling. Back.

'Okay,' Soli whispers, 'okay. We could face them down but . . .'

Tidge takes over: 'we're kids not super-heroes and this is real life.'

The nerve-rash Mouse gets is claiming his face. 'The bathroom's scaring me like crazy, guys,' he warns. 'What went on, before, in the bath, it's got scratches like something was trying to get out and, and . . .' He can't go on.

'Didn't,' Tidge concludes. Neither has been to the loo all morning in fact.

'The bed,' Soli commands. They scramble under it. She drags down the duvet to cover the gap between the mattress and floor and Mouse finds his brother's hand and they wait with trembly breaths.

Footsteps. Hesitating. Changing direction. Heading to the bed. Closer. Closer. They stop. The cover's grabbed. Tugged. Your daughter yanks back. The boys are now gripping each other so tight Mouse's fingernails are digging into Tidge's palms and there is blood in tiny sickles. Tidge can feel its sticky wet—

'*Why* do you lot always have to make everything so difficult?'

The duvet's dropped. Three little faces peer out. Burst into laughter.

It's B.

B! They are safe, they are safe and you sink to your knees

with relief unfurling in your chest. Motl's protégé, surrogate son, closest friend.

'Um, sorry, guys,' says your daughter, 'love you lots but there's something I've got to do.'

She dashes to the bathroom.

'Hurry up!' Mouse wails, then Tidge.

'La la la,' she sings back.

Whatever one expects, things turn out otherwise.

∽ 41 ∾

The family cook, from long ago. When people like that were allowed. When you lived in your sparkly suburb, when Project Indigo consumed your life. But after the servants were long gone B kept bobbing up out of the blue, banging on the door of Salt Cottage and hollering for any grown-up to scat and yes yes, yada yada, the carrots would be mixed in with the bolognese sauce and the kids would be in bed by eight. And you knew he'd be teaching them to turn eyelids inside out and do the alphabet in burps, but Motl and you obeyed for they adored him, his stories and tickles and teasing and jokes, and it was a blessed circuit-break; a release, from the *intensity* of parenthood, for a couple of hours at least. He always outstayed his welcome and never went home when he should, as if he was always trying to slip into your family, as if there was nothing else. His mantra is that there are only three ways to live now: to participate, flee, or transcend. And he chooses to transcend. 'With kids. Any I can get.'

And now, and now, it is time to surrender to trust.

Because B is Motl's unmovable choice in this. The unlikely saviour: 'Have some faith, Mrs, have some faith.' But you're just not sure about this man now embedded in your kids' life.

Yet in that pale space right now, well, everything is upended, and you can only smile at that. Your children are suddenly in a dear white balloon of a room all hazy with a lemony light and the sun is bursting through clouds like tent ropes from heaven and life is good, so good, in this place. Certainty has spread through all three of them like parachutes floating them, gently, to the ground. Soli is renewed. Radiant. She hates not knowing, just like you; everything, always, has to be under control and now B is here and he's a thread to her parents and everything is okay and she can hand over responsibility and her face is ironed out.

Examine everything carefully. Hold fast to that which is good.

42

'*Why* should I trust him?' you interrogated Motl once. 'Give me one reason.'

He propped his fingertips under his chin. 'Because, Mrs, he's extremely clever. He's able to flit between many worlds. And we're damned lucky he's on our side.'

'That's what you say.'

'I'm as close to a father as he'll get. He doesn't have one. His dad said to him on his eighth birthday that he could no longer touch him, kiss him good night – he was a man now. And twenty years later, when his father was taking his last breaths, B grabbed him and hugged him. I've been wanting to do this for years, he told him, and both men wept. We've wept together, my love, many times since. You don't do that with many men.'

'Right,' you say slowly.

'He's got courage and we need that. He's a lion of a fighter, an independent thinker. That's very important in this world. He's his own man.'

On that point, yes. B always seems more alive than everyone else; a room always seems lit when he's in it. He's got a quick, wiry boy-body but everything else about him is big: the energy, enthusiasm, spark. His past is a fist balled shut but Motl doesn't care: 'It's in his face, *look*, it's incapable of cruelty and there are so few faces in the world like that.' You're not so sure. You've said more than once that your husband's an old cashmere sock, too soft, and that people like him could, possibly, be blinded by B like a camera flash bleeding the world out. Because he now works for the new regime, as a chef, to various people high up, and he shouldn't be mixing with the likes of you lot. 'He's fine, relax,' is always Motl's response. 'He's the only person in the world I now trust. Well, besides the trouble and strife.'

'It's wartime, mate,' you respond fiercely, 'and in wartime you don't know who to trust.'

And so B is the reason behind Motl's firming of heart on that final, rain-lashed night. Your three precious children are now in this man's hands. And you have to soften, you have to soften and unclench at the thought of that.

I drew them with bands of love.

∽ 43 ∽

'Okay, team. Everything okay here? No shark bites? Knocks?'

Soli shakes her head with sparkly eyes and B ruffles her hair with his familiar dirty grin, one side up, one side down, and something tightens in your heart. Tidge gets a wink.

'So this is where you work?' Mouse asks. 'Cool, the last place anyone would look—'

He stops. Hang on, *no*, you lean in, to the cogs of his thinking, all your anxieties soaked through him too much. Because their supposed family friend is nestled into the heart of the new regime. He works in the most notorious building in the country, a place where people disappear and never come back. A place Mum and Dad talk about deep into the night with no light in their voices. 'Is this where I think it is?' Mouse asks.

B nods.

'Where are Mum and Dad?' Mouse asks.

B smiles, shakes his head.

Mouse wipes his hand across his mouth, fear now capsizing everything. He steps back. Mind uncurling. Is this a cage? Are they bait? Is *this* how they get the grown-ups to talk?

'How did we get in here, B?' Yes, how?

A pink sphere of gum emerges from his lips, is smartly popped and efficiently sucked back. 'This, my lovelies,' he replies nonchalantly, 'is my best story yet. Once upon a time there were three potato crates. Mighty big ones. And a delivery truck for the kitchen that was signed off by the master chef. Oh, and before that there was a boat. A little one that almost sank.' He's all cackly with his cleverness. 'But it worked, guys, it worked!'

'From Salt Cottage?' Mouse. Cold, incredulous. 'But boats can't get to it. It's too rough.'

'Trust – your – B.' The man smiles. 'There's an awful lot you don't know about him, mate.'

And as he talks there's a fragment, déjà vu, from when, you don't know, you're so tired, can't work it out; but a last glance, to the beach, to three imprints of tiny bodies pressed into the sand, in a row; three joyous angels like snow angels and children's footprints leading down to them *but not back.* As if three little bodies had been magicked from your land by the sky or the sea but of course, the high tide mark, yes, that would work and you shake your head trying to shake sense from it but no, how, can't, too tired, everything hurts.

For they are removed from hearing the discourse of angels.

∞ 44 ∞

'Why were we put to sleep?' Mouse is not letting up.

'Because we couldn't risk you being awake.'

'Why?'

B sweeps up his twin brother and locks his arms around his legs. 'Because your dad knew you'd never get into the boat, you'd never accept an escape by sea. Without them. You were far too terrified of all the stories you'd heard and your dad said your little hearts might just stop, with fright. And he also thought that back on land, if any of you woke up in the boxes, you'd be all bouncy and snuffly like a bunch of kittens and you'd give the game away. I had to go through several road-blocks and if any of you so much as sneezed they weren't too sure you'd be able to talk your way out. For me, you were much better off asleep.' He glares playfully at Tidge, your boy who has a need to be loved, by everyone, which means he's never wily enough with his talk. He's far too innocent for this world, his heart's too wide open; people like him always get crushed. He squirms in embarrassment.

'Why weren't we told where we were going, B?' Mouse is not finished yet.

'Because perhaps if you knew, *some* of you might not have come. Some of you might have chosen to remain at Salt Cottage ... which wasn't for the best.'

'Why aren't they with us?'

'They're extremely busy right now. They'll be back.'

'Put my brother down.'

His little mind going like a windmill in a hurricane and the ends of your fingers tingling as if all the blood is draining from them and pooling in a panic in your heart because B's face is suddenly set; in an instant the atmosphere is changed, like sun snatched by cloud.

Tidge's now struggling in his arms to get down, get out, and B's blowing another bubble right in his face and there's no smile, no warmth and Tidge doesn't blink. '*Please* put me down,' he pleads.

'That's what I was waiting for, Mr.' He's floated gently to the ground. B looks closely at all your children. Stripped, suddenly, of any silliness.

'There was nowhere else to go,' he says in another voice entirely. 'No safe house left. This room was the only choice. I wasn't able to tell your father that.'

The room hushes like a blanket has dropped over it.

Did not our heart burn within us while he talked with us?

❧ 45 ❧

You gaze at them and gaze at them like a curiosity-crazed tourist from a glass-bottomed boat, willing them on and holding out trembling palms; holding them strong and calming on the blades of their pale, fragile backs.

Keep on sculpting light.

∽ 46 ∾

But B. He looks different. Shinier. Scrubbed. The leather jacket is gone, and the biker boots he's worn his entire adult life, and the struggle of a beard always light on his chin that shouts of the little boy who's never grown up. He used to look tetherless, a wild pony, but now he looks tamed and it's wrong. He's in uniform. His hair's severely combed. He doesn't look any more like the family friend who loudly magicked sweets from ears and theme tunes from pianos; he looks like someone else.

The new lot.

As if the old B's been stolen and replaced.

Mouse clamps his hand at his mouth as if he's going to be sick. 'When are we getting out? What are those noises in the night? Where are Mum and Dad? What's happening, *what*?'

But the man Motl trusts with his life – and his children's – is ignoring all the talk, he's backing out fast, singing cheerily that he'll be returning soon with some food and not to worry, just wait.

But leaving a tumble of questions churning, churning in his wake.

Rough is the road.

✂ 47 ✂

Tidge flops on the bed. 'Food glorious food,' he cackles.

Mouse looks across in despair: he's not getting it. G rattles the key and he swivels at the efficient click and spins and spins the doorknob then stalks to the one person who may, just may, know something about what's going on. '*What* is happening?'

But Soli's face is closed for business, the shutters are down, it can't be read. Her shoulders are tight like she's battening down an explosive force, some fearful secret she'll never let out. She turns to the vaulting sky, to the stately migration of clouds and sucks a stem of hair furiously, as if it holds the taste of home; of certainty and parents and a rightful childhood when everything was all right and she didn't have to do this.

'*Tell* us!' her brother commands.

Soli leans further to the sky.

He holds his palms to his head and begins to yell in frustration.

'Be patient, you,' she says calmly, 'we've made it. We're safe. Be grateful for what you've got.'

Mouse covers his ears trying to shut the know-it-all out because his sister's not in the habit of saying be patient, you, in that silky mummy voice, she's not entitled to it yet. He grabs a chunk of her hair with an explosion of savage intent. Pulls. She screams. Strands break. 'Well, that's the split ends dealt with,' he declares in triumph.

His sister punches him, equally as violent, yelling that their father wanted them to stay put and listen to B and that's all she knows, all she was told and you know why? 'Because he didn't want us doing anything we shouldn't. Like running away. Or not listening. Or pulling hair. *Brat.*'

Mouse comes back for more, kicking and punching his sister, all feralled up. 'Tell us what's going on, *tell us.*'

She's had enough. 'That's all you're good for, isn't it? Biting and scratching. Nothing *useful.* You, you . . . *thing.* You weren't meant to be born. You weren't meant to be with us. The doctor said you weren't worth it. Never forget that.'

Silence, as if the air itself has flinched.

Your three children stare at each other in horror, at the words coming out, at everything soured up so fast. Oh, girl girl girl. She always has that arrow-aim of swift, attacking talk. And she's right. You were told to abort the second twin in utero, it was feeding off the healthy child's food supply, it would save the bigger one; 'it was for the best.' You couldn't. That tiny heart, beating so fast, that fierce little life. The *insistence* of it. You'd had a miscarriage two months before their conception and you'll never forget the swamping, crippling grief of it. 'Cry, and cry again,' the nurse told you gently as your womb was being scraped out. 'It's a bereavement, love.' Oh yes.

The boys were never supposed to know but your daughter found out, and let it slip. And in the howl of the learning you rocked your younger boy and kissed the beautiful double cream of the back of his neck, you nuzzled that warm, soft nape and told him he was wanted so fiercely, so much. But he wailed over and over, 'Mummy doesn't love me.'

'No, darling, sssh, you're here because we love you so much.'

But from that day onwards your daughter's words have been like a splinter under his skin that can never be pulled out, a hurt that will never stop. And what do you know, it's all been freshened up.

'Where *are* they?' Mouse wails to her now, defeated, the only question left he can push out.

'I don't know,' she replies, exhausted.

The boys know she's speaking the truth.

A new silence, thick.

As they take it in.

The enormousness of the alone.

In this parent-bleached place.

What we speak becomes the house we live in.

∽ 48 ∾

'I bet this was Dad's idea,' says Mouse, later. 'He's so kind of, you know, *trusting*.'

His siblings look at him dubiously.

'Oh, forget it.' He sighs.

I think I've reached somewhere I shouldn't have TWENTY YEARS TOO SOON.

Despite yourself you laugh.

His sister stalks to the bathroom; his brother speaks soothingly in her wake. 'You *heard* B. There was nowhere else. No safe house left.'

Mouse sighs and sits cross-legged on the bed. 'I want to resign from the lot of you,' he announces, shutting his eyes and trying to coax calm back.

'A feast is com-ing, dude,' Tidge teases.

Mouse rubs his head as if his brain has wound down with the great dumping wave of stress and tired at being in this place. Tidge doubles over. It's been a long time since food.

I'm STARVING. And I've never felt more alone in my life. It shines glittery bright. In this enormous, waiting quiet.

So. Here they are. Each in a little universe of their own and hasn't it happened quick. The silence between them is soiled and how you despair at that. At the vicious hurt only family can inflict.

Anger sinks the boat.

∽ 49 ∾

B's back. Wheeling in a trolley with three silver domes all sweating with impatience and announcing he'll be coming every day, around this time, and before anyone can say, hang on, every *day*? he's out the door with a triumphant click of the key in the lock. The kids stare at the trolley as if it's a Trojan horse. At the silver domes waiting to be plucked off. At the strawberry milkshakes deflating in thick glass.

Silence.

Tidge takes a sniff. 'Chicken, guys.' He circles, hands behind his back like a judge at an agricultural show. He plucks a dome. 'Rice. Warm bread. Mangoes and custard for dessert.' He tugs his brother's elbow. 'Come on, *you*, Mum and Dad have planned it.'

'How do you know?'

'Because, *der*, they're the only people in the world who know exactly what our favourite foods are, and they're all here.'

'It could be poisoned.'

You've got to be kidding, says Tidge's face. Soli's had enough. She grabs Mouse's arm and marches him forward with that enthusiasm for doing she's had since birth that's as persistent as rust and can't be shaken off. All he can do is sigh, in the manner of people who wear black turtlenecks. Who he says he's going to be when he grows up because those kinds of people never do sport. Or what others want. Tidge throws a bread roll at him and cackles. The energy between them is all wrong. He's one of those people who's been blasted with life; as for Mouse, it's like it has to be fed through him with an intravenous drip.

'Mum and Dad ordered the custard just for you, mate.' Tidge laughs. 'And it's about to be delivered,' as he flicks it onto his brother's face and licks it off then declares that there's no one to wipe their lips with spit on a tissue or tell them to close their mouth when they chew so what are they waiting for, come *on*, bro, come on!

My religion is very simple. My religion is kindness.

❦ 50 ❦

Mouse suddenly dives in, hunger getting the better of him. His siblings cheer as he works his way from the custard first to the rice last and then one by one they flop back onto the bed, and laugh. Basking for a moment in the fabulousness of transcending; believing, for a moment, in that Salt Cottage certainty: that everything will be all right. Because yes, the table's soaked in their parents' gleeful touch. So yes, they must have planned it. And yes, the three of them are hidden away in here, warm and safe.

Your youngest burps in satisfaction (the little bugger) and now they're all doing it (the little buggers) and no one's stopping them and they're suddenly laughing endlessly, can't stop. Tidge's then singing 'Food, Glorious Food' in burps and placing a silver dome on his head and now they're all marching around the room and clanging the domes with knives and jumping on the bed because no one is stopping them and they can, they can. The three of them finally crash onto the mattress in a jumbly heap and are quiet, breathing deep, and their little cage of a room suddenly has such a tranquillity soaked into it, like a place where you're put to recover and rest, to clean yourself of the past. A metre from this room the grown-up world starts but not here, not now, not yet. This, for the moment, is the wonder house. Sanctified by joy.

Tidge gets all cackly again. Turns to his brother and hugs him and as he clamps him tight he whispers, 'Mummy,' then again, urgently, 'Mummy,' catching the smell of you, your gardenia perfume, on his brother's skin and clothes and hair. It's everywhere, as if you've rolled each of them in your love before letting them go, like flour into dough, folding it through them.

'I can feel her here,' Tidge whispers in wonder.

'Me too,' Soli says, 'she's like salt in a fishing village. All over the place.'

She turns in that vivid air but you've caught it. Her eyes blinking like a semaphore signal. The crack in the mask.

They stand not still, they never close their eyelids,
those sentinels of Gods who wander round us.

☙ 51 ❧

B returns for the trolley. Takes a backpack from his shoulder. Throws it at Mouse. An adult throw. Hard at his chest. Your boy fails to catch it. This is not unusual. He's never caught in his life anything except chicken pox. He's always the last one left as the sports teams are being picked, knows too searingly well that smile of not-caring that becomes stretched and aching and tight. As your heart breaks. B's someone who's always picked first. It's in his smile and his walk. You're not sure what his game is now and you bristle in defence.

You've never been sure the man likes you. Perhaps it's a jealousy over your husband, or perhaps something else. You suspect he knows of Project Indigo. Just occasionally, a too keen glance when you walked into the room with a sheaf of papers, or a nonchalant question about work. You can't imagine Motl telling him. From some other source, perhaps; whispers, or something worse: briefing notes. You wish, *wish* you could surrender to trust.

'Spare clothes, team,' he announces now.

Tidge plucks out his favourite *Star Wars* T-shirt. 'Two sets of everything,' he says slowly, thinking it through, 'so in two days we'll be out. Yippeeee!'

'You won't be here long,' is the only response. And too curt for your liking. He never talks in that tone when you're around. He takes a book and an old doll from a shopping bag. The toy wears a sailor suit, its china head has no hair left, just holes and one eye is skewed like a toddler's dug in fierce. Mouse looks at it warily: it belongs too much to someone else. The leather cover of the book is blackened by age and an enormous brass clasp seals it defensively shut. These things would never belong in their mucky, crayon-scuffed house; they're too strange and remote. 'The book is for Soli. The doll for Tidge. If we got this far' – B's voice bunkers down – 'I was to give them to you.' He hands a tiny key to Soli. 'For the book.'

'What about me? What do I get? No fair,' Mouse cries.

'Check your pocket, scribe.'

The pen. Of course. With its mission attached. A smile fills up Mouse. B ruffles his hair. 'You, Mr, landed the jackpot. That pen is one of your father's most precious things in the world. Besides me. Oh, and you lot.'

Your boy glows, blinks, tears gathering at the gate. Kindness is breaking him, finally, and you soften. Perhaps, just perhaps your Motl is right.

THIS REPORT WON'T BE STOPPED UNTIL MUM AND DAD WALK BACK INTO IT. I promise, Dad. I'll show you I can do it, you just watch.

Strong, he writes into the night. Motl knew exactly what he was doing with that pen. Little Mouse is the child who always says he can't do anything, is hopeless, is not good enough. His father has given him this task because he knows he can do it, and do it well; he is giving him the gift of esteem.

*We should support each other, give more warmth,
in such a demanding world as this.*

❦ 52 ❦

Day three. The stillness hour, 5 a.m., the hour when voices carry furthest. 'Where are the boys?' Tidge's asking again as he stares out of the window at the emptiness of the street.

'I don't know,' Mouse replies, from the bed, the sheet a sweaty rope about him. 'It's too early. Forget it.'

Tidge can't. It's in his arms that are shawling his shoulders tight, and his pale fingers that are tightly clutching his flesh. His exuberance has been extinguished in this room, his silly, charming spark, and you all need it so much.

'Come back to bed, matey,' Soli pleads.

Eventually, taking his time, Tidge pads across. An arm from his sister and a leg from his brother lock over him.

But his eyes. Wide awake.

A merry heart doeth good like a medicine.

∽ 53 ∽

What you all need: Tidge's bubbly shine. Soli singing into her hairbrush when she thinks she's alone. Mouse's astonishingly pure whistling that enslaves anyone who listens, when he's happy, when he's completely absorbed in a task. The talking-dark tonic of the magic house, its endless swish of sea and sky crowding the air.

Not this. An unnatural silence so quiet it hums.

You slam your eyes shut on mornings when the boys would wake Motl and you with their high sunny voices springing into the day and then they'd thunder across to your room and clamber onto your bed and you'd both clamp pillows over your heads but they'd drag them off and burrow into your laughing, protesting warmth. You slam your eyes shut on that rich, rich world. That time with your family was like God breathing life into the spirit-sapped bellows of your days and making everything alive and light. That great incandescence, vanished. For now you stand in a great cavernous stillness and the room waits in response. Just the selfishness of your ambition, your choice, all that's left.

Silence like mould.

You want oysters. Want to throw back your head and swallow the sea. Want singing that rises heavenward, challenging the ceiling. Want to fling open your night windows with the lights blazing and marvel at so much wanting in: moths and midges, wind and sea and salt. Want to burrow deep into the envelope of your soil and smell the lovely grass. Want to be locked in sunshine. You come from a big sky place and now you have never loved the world so much. All the outrageous beauty of it. Want your Motl, impish and gleeful and full of juice, his touch as he slips into bed long after you've fallen into sleep and you stir and he curls around you in a moment of cherishing and chuff. Now now now. Touch is everything and you have left the house of touch. How you imagine Salt Cottage at this moment: taut, holding its breath; no children to bang and clatter life into it; windows firmly shut; no noise, no life.

The silence here is a presence. It waits.

Stay close to any sounds that make you glad you are alive.

❧ 54 ❧

A day so still it seems stunned. 'It must be Sunday,' Tidge murmurs, trying to work it out. 'Hang on, no, I – I've lost count.'

You too. Your brain is winding down. The children are clotted at the window, pale and translucent. They haven't been grubby for so long, proper grubby of black under fingernails and sunshine sweat and mud silky soft. Which is the opposite of stillness, which is now.

'The doll doesn't look worried,' Tidge says, peering at it quizzically.

The sky hangs sullen, the colour of wet slate on a roof. Thunder skips across it like a series of bombs being dropped. The tree outside shivers. Mouse peels away.

Wish list: Air that's got no complication in it. Like at home.

The waiting now is like a dog with its head on its paws. 'Trust,' Soli whispers, her hand resting lightly on Tidge's hip, 'just trust.'

The sun bursts momentarily through cloud. He smiles. Tugs on the heavy curtains. Swings. Laughs in delight. Your boy's back!

He's joined. By Mouse, whooping, 'To stop the thinking, all right,' and suddenly the three of them are bouncing off the walls in this place, trampolining on the bed, doing handstands against the walls. And it feels like the first time your youngest has ever done anything remotely resembling physical activity and your daughter says it's ironic that his arrival in the real world should coincide with being in this place, in which the real world has been left behind.

'Temp-o-rarily,' Tidge chants, 'temp-o-rarily!' Glee smiling them up, and yourself.

It has not rained light for many days.

≈ 55 ≈

Soli pulls the boys into a sit. They're in front of the doll. She's placed it on the floor in front of them. Mouse is uninterested, he attempts to stand. He's tugged back.

'I have to tell you something about it. It's really important. It could be the key to getting out of here. We have to believe that.'

'Okay.' Tidge nods.

His head is wide open but Mouse's alarm bells are going off, he's squirming, wants escape. He's the cynic of the family, the watcher, the survivor; he'll make a good critic, you laugh. Aged six he asked if we made God or God made us then declared he knew the answer – us – and you applauded his rationalism and encouraged it.

Soli now places any stray hands she can get onto her knees, attempting to corral all the skittery thinking. 'Dad said I have to tell you to look at the doll, to help us.'

Yeah, right, says Mouse's wriggle.

'He promised he'll come back and get us. And when we look at it, we always have to remember that. He *promised* me.'

But there's a fierceness in those last three words that sits her brother up straight.

If even a dog's tooth is truly worshipped it glows with light.

❧ 56 ❧

'It's like we teach our children what we want to believe,' Motl said once, deep into the night, 'then we see that they have this beautiful faith and it helps them go to bed peacefully and get a good night's sleep – and meanwhile we're off in the other room not sleeping at all. But it's worth it, I think.'

_I think we are frightened every moment of our lives
until we know him._

∞ 57 ∞

'Imagine we're home.' Quiet congregates as Soli weaves her spell of words. 'Mum's singing as she washes down the windows, Dad's tinkering under the bonnet of the car. You're riding his bike. You know, how you do – Tidge's on the seat pedalling and Mouse is side-saddle steering and you're whizzing down the drive and Mum's laughing because she's singing her mad songs, like she's permanently twenty-three again, she's got her face back.' They all smile. Being twenty-three was your little joke whenever anyone asked your age, in the time when you'd sing every moment that you could, loudly and off-key and with all the wrong words. 'You're home, guys, safe,' your daughter continues, 'and we'll have it again. Dad promised.'

You sense Mouse uncurling, loosening, even . . . believing. That they're not alone, that this is all part of some grand plan. His eyes blink open to a room expectant and still and hushed, like a candle lit.

'But he said we'll only be able to endure all this if we leave our fear behind. If we trust. And we have to be appreciators. We have to be grateful for what we've got because if we're grateful, we're content. And from that . . . apparently' – she falters – 'comes strength.'

The three of them stay sitting in that room as pale as breath for goodness knows how long, brought down into stillness, feeling righted, lit. The day feels newly clean. Washed. Possibility unfolding before them. You sit back. Shake your head, smile.

See now a fragment of your husband's plan. The biologist in him ruminated once that religion is about enduring, in a survival-of-the-fittest sense. 'Maybe it gives you strength. Maybe we're programmed by evolution to have belief. Perhaps it's in our genes.'

Mouse's eyes spring open. 'But Dad's cling,' he whispers, 'it's with me too much. I can't.'

He jerks up his head as if he senses, in the prickle of his skin, he's being watched.

You wear the stillness of his gaze like a thumbprint.

Haply thou wearest thyself away with grief because thou believe not.

⧼ 58 ⧽

'Why are you doing this, B?' Mouse's suspicion is now ransacking everything.

'I love striding off into the great unknown. Don't you, Mr?'

'Um, well, we're not striding.'

B knocks on his head. No response. Tickles under the arms. No response. Mouse's fencing himself off, he's had enough. He's now got the measure of this Peter Pan man who's always distracting them with some new trick. Your kids are now wound up as tight as tin toys and the only magic that's going to work any more is getting them out. And parents back.

B squats in front of your flinty scowly boy. Holds him firmly by the shoulders and whispers, adult to adult, that whoever saves one life saves the world entire and runs his finger down his face then leaves, shutting them away like a coat no longer needed for warmth. Mouse bangs frustratedly on the door behind him. You bite your lip. 'A face that's incapable of cruelty,' Motl insisted, yes, but your babies are now being cemented into this room and of all the hiding places in the world they shouldn't be here, in this place.

You had to obey your husband, had to surrender to this. Because *you* had no way of saving them, no ally, no plan. He did. And even though you have a totally different perception of B you had to relinquish control to Motl. Because he loves these children as much as you do. And you are the liability here.

> *Tranquil sage is he who, steadfast, walks alone,*
> *unmoved by blame and by praise.*

❧ 59 ❧

A low butter moon pulls Mouse from sleep and he stands at the window and a prickling comes over him. 'Mummy?' he whispers. He takes out his notebook, breathing fast.

She's close.

He looks across to his brother, to his face tight and troubled in restless sleep.

Perhaps she's RIGHT HERE. In this building. AND Dad.

Mouse gasps, Tidge wakes. Mouse jumps under the covers. 'I don't trust B,' he says firmly, matter-of-fact.

'Me too, dude,' his brother replies and Mouse looks at him in wonder: perhaps his cynicism is finally rubbing off.

The cover's furiously yanked. 'He could be just amazingly clever, guys.' Soli. Irritable. 'He never gets questioned, or disappeared, or detained. Have you ever noticed that?'

'I just *hate* all the silliness,' Mouse wails.

Their sister holds up her hands in mock prayer. 'Well, may he never grow up.'

'Soli's got a boyfriend, Soli's got a boyfriend,' both boys chant.

She grabs her pillow with a hrumph and curls like a carpet beetle on the floor. 'It's *really hard* being the only grown-up in this place,' she wails. Shivering.

Mouse gets out of bed.

Walks to the cupboard.

Finds the spare blanket and throws it over his sister.

She looks up in disbelief. Smiles.

And now it is the turn of your own eyes to blink like a semaphore signal. Because as a parent generosity is the most important lesson you can teach your children, because from generosity springs everything else.

A soul waking up.

∞ 60 ∞

But Mouse. Still unable to catch on to sleep. Staring out at the clouds racing and the moon watching, as if the sky is fleeing. Finally falling into a dirty, scrappy, dishwater slumber and tossing and turning, his notebook splayed beside him.

Soli says we're here for our safety. Right. That Mum and Dad couldn't tell us because we never would have gone with B, never would have left them. But too huge in my head is Mum's watery 'mmm' when I asked her once if B was our friend. 'Your father thinks so, yes.' Too huge in my head is Mum saying, then again perhaps he's an angel; what does she know? Perhaps he's cleaving into our family for warmth because he doesn't have any family himself. Too huge in my head is Dad chattering on about how we should always be kind to other people because we never know when we're entertaining angels unaware. Too huge in my head is Mum spinning Tidge around and lifting his shirt and holding his shoulder blades and saying, 'See, look, this is where our angel's wings once were,' then sliding her hands around his tummy and keeping them there for a very long time and bowing her head, and going very still.

She's here. Close.

<u>*Then a spirit passed before my face*</u>
<u>*and the hair of my flesh stood up.*</u>

112

❧ 61 ❧

Proper feral now, wilder versions of themselves. Like abandoned houses where nature has run rampant. A river-map of dirty lines on their palms, matted hair clotting into dreadlocks, clothes they can't be bothered to wash. As grimy and greasy as worn bank notes. It'll be war-paint next, blood on the cheeks. Mouse sniffles. A cold's coming on. Tidge says it's his body crying; Soli says shut up, you lot, you have to stay strong. She never gets colds. She's such a pirate of a girl, always battling on; it's in her chin, its perky point, and the set of her mouth. 'I wish I could infect you,' Mouse grumbles and breathes hard into her face.

Oh, guys.

He keeps looking across at the old volume on the windowsill. The book muncher of the family hasn't dared a touch. As if he's terrified of what it may hold, the certainty of what it may impart. Your child who's knotted by complexity, so complicated, tight; for all his cynicism he hates novelty and adventure and risk, for all his pushing away he needs you so much. His little hand used to lock over your throat whenever you lay next to him to lull him to sleep. 'I'm holding on to you so you can't run away from the beddy-byes,' he whispered once. 'I've got the mummy disease, you have to stay close.'

He goes up to the old book now, hovers a touch, retreats.

Hold this book close to your heart
for it contains wonderful secrets.

❧ 62 ❧

A bomb. Somewhere in the wings of outside. Far enough away but still the twins cower on the floor with their arms wrapped over their heads. Another. A siren insisting. And then it is over, the aftermath. The children rush to the window. A soldier's footsteps pound past then a child's. 'Wow!' Tidge shouts. Raggedy trousers flit by and there's a cheeky yell and a flash of a smile and your kids crane their heads but all they catch is a tangle of hair and pyjama trousers under shorts and a white balloon being tugged on a string and they all laugh at the clean, crazy, up-yours joy of that, so bizarre and happy and fragile in this place.

'Who was he?' Tidge asks.

'Maybe he's from some old abandoned house.' Soli smiles. 'Filled with a huge gang of kids who flit about in the shadows, scavenging for food, playing jacks with the knucklebones of soldiers—'

'*Safe*,' Mouse butts in, craning his head at the window. 'Let's find them, guys. It's no use waiting any more. We've *got* to get out.'

'But Dad,' Soli protests, 'what if he comes and we're not here?'

None of them can answer that.

You've all heard the stories. Feral kids. Caught in the city's cracks. Lairs of lost children who've been stained by the world, with eyes that are old because they've seen too much. The trunk of the tree outside glows golden with the last of the day and the world for a moment catches its breath. Everything, suddenly, is weighty with the loveliness of the light; the blank, shining windows of the building opposite, the tree, the sky. Your kids' existence has shrunk to this untouchable beauty, another child's whoop and his joyous footsteps, their dying out.

Suddenly, insistently, irrepressible hope.

And the light shineth in darkness,
and the darkness comprehendeth it not.

❧ 63 ❧

B backs in fast. Spilling cutlery from the trolley, not bothering to pick it up. The table's piled high but there are no silver domes, not even a white cloth. Something big's up. The kids find each other's hands. B turns. Takes a breath, doesn't want to say what's coming next. He has to go away. They'll have enough to eat – a last-minute thing – only two days.

Mouse steps back. 'But you seem . . . *afraid*.' Because he's nervy, trembly, like a horse before a race.

Soli leaps in. 'What's happening? Where are you going?'

B holds up his hands, shielding his face.

'What if there's a fire?' Tidge. Sitting calmly under the window, holding the doll. And he has a point, a good one.

'Yes, a fire, we need a key!' Mouse.

'Imagine if we're stuck,' Soli insists, 'we'll burn to death.'

B looks from one to the other as if they're the most morbidly strange children he's ever met. He takes the key from his pocket with a deep, doubting breath. Wipes the back of his hand across his lips. 'This can *only* be used in an emergency. You can't go outside. For anything else.'

The kids nod, saucer-eyed.

B walks to the book and places the key carefully on it. 'You'll *never* see your mum and dad again if something goes wrong.' He shuts the door behind him and instantly opens it again. 'Whoops, I need the key to lock you in, don't I?' He laughs nervously – he never laughs nervously – and his lopsided grin is not quite right, it's too stiffly in place with a wobble in his lip, a new tic. He snatches the key and backs out. Locks them in. It shoots under the door as if alive with a force of its own.

The kids stare. Hesitate. Lunge.

Soli wins. Of course. She holds the key to her chest and rises on her toes like a pint-sized Mary Poppins about to swoop off a clear foot from the ground – Tidge shuts his eyes and chants, 'Please don't sing, please don't sing' – then she drops to her heels with a defeated thud. 'Mum and Dad,' she whispers fearfully. 'We *can't.*'

'I'll mind it if you want,' Tidge volunteers, all sweetness and light.

His sister looks at him like yeah, right.

Do not seek refuge in anyone but yourselves.

❧ 64 ❧

Tidge's nose is pressed to the door. 'It smells pretty good out there, guys.' A cheeky grin.

Mouse knows what it means.

Soli too. 'No, no, no.' She wags her finger.

'I was only commentating,' Tidge huffs. 'I'm going to be a private investigator when I grow up. I'm in training.'

'Uh-huh.' She takes the key from her pocket. Rises. '*No*,' she whispers to herself, slipping it back.

'I'm still starving.' Tidge rolls onto his back, laughing, rubbing his stomach.

He's now circling the trolley. Dividing everything into three. 'B's left an awful lot of peanuts. And the bananas are going spotty. And the apples have bruises. There's not much that's useful here, actually. He wasn't thinking or was in an awful rush or—'

'He's done it deliberately,' Mouse concludes.

'Stop it, boys, stop it.'

'I'm hun-greeeeee.' Tidge, later.

'What's that, lovie?' Mouse, holding a hugely theatrical hand to his ear.

'I'm *HUN-GREEEEEEE*,' Tidge giggles back.

Soli buries her head in her hands and groans. Despite your-self you laugh, remembering those golden days at Salt Cottage when it was like the four of them existed on this earth to bring laughter into your life; your beautiful, buoyant coterie; all those days burnished with them. The varnish of them all, glowing you alive, and you are so thankful for that no matter what your existence is now because you lived, truly lived, once.

And the day star arise in your hearts.

⤲ 65 ⤳

'Why couldn't *I* have been the perfect one? The one who's . . . cherished.' Mouse watches Soli pacing the room like a dog in the back of a stationary pick-up.

'The squeaky wheel on the bike always gets the attention, mate,' she responds, fierce, like he should get it. 'They never worry about me. *I* never get any hovering. And I don't look like any of you guys, either.' You lean; there's a pale, soft underbelly in her voice that she rarely allows out. 'Maybe I was adopted.' Tremulous, younger than she's sounded for years. Oh, love. She's blue-eyed and black-haired and none of the rest of you are but it means nothing and you need to tell her, enfold her in your arms; need to tell her how vividly different all your three children are and it constantly amazes you. Need to tell her that when you were pregnant with her Motl would put his hand on the drum of your belly and a calmness would bloom through you; need to tell her that as a tiny baby she taught you to relinquish control, to shed selfishness, and you're so grateful for that.

'You've got Mum's laugh,' Tidge says brightly. That boy. It's as if he's permanently surrounded by bluebells and daisies when there's not a bluebell or daisy in sight.

'Not lately, mate.'

'Well, we could all do with it back,' Mouse says by way of apology.

A soft quiet. Peace at last. They need this. When the twins

were in utero they'd jump awake when they heard Soli's toddler cry, so blood-bound, all of them, and over the years the fundamental force of that has been lost. Perhaps, perhaps, this room can knit it back.

Mouse flops down on the bed and opens out his arms. A cuddle's needed. 'Sis?' He clings then pulls her off in alarm. 'Where are you?' Running his hands over her skinniness, feeling her bones, the jittery pulse of her flesh. And the bananas going off, and the apples bruised, and two days now up.

Engineers fashion wells, carpenters fashion wood,
the wise fashion themselves.

✂ 66 ✂

Okay. The deal. I DO NOT want my skeleton found in this cupboard, thank you very much. I do not want ants delirious at my flesh.

Three days since B left. His food hasn't lasted as long as it should.

Wish list: a full belly. A lovely snuggly roll in Mum's laughing. Air as crisp as an apple bite.

Mouse gazes out of the window and sighs. Buds are on the bare tree, the air outside is lightening, the cold's beginning to unclench.

'It still smells good out there,' Tidge throws in from the door. He's got all fancied-up today, in his good clothes: red checked shirt, jeans with the knees out.

Mouse straightens his brother's collar and wipes a soap smear from his face. 'Anyone we know?' he teases.

Tidge lifts him in a hug. 'Does it still smell good to you, dude? Is it a smell you could trust?'

'He could be just minutes away.' Soli throws a warning across the bows of the room. But both boys have caught a telltale chink in her voice.

'Ah-ha!' Tidge cries, triumphant. 'So you're starving too, eh sis?'

'Something must have gone wrong,' she says, quiet. 'He said to stay put,' quieter still.

Mouse throws in that maybe this was planned. Weeks ago. 'It needs to be said.'

Soli takes the key from her pocket and places it next to the doll and kneads her right temple just as you used to when a migraine attacked.

'I can't bear this,' Tidge declares, hands on his hips. And with a lunge he grabs the key and walks out. Locks the door behind him, swiftly and cleanly, like a sail on a yacht snapping free from its rope.

'I won't be long,' he yells from the other side.

Gone. Gone. Gone.

Just like that.

*The sensible man is not influenced by
what other people think.*

⤳ 67 ⤳

Your boy your boy your boy. You cannot see him, he is lost. You flap your fingers at your face like you've eaten something hot. Disbelief. Panic. Anger. That he could be so disobedient. 'This might just work.' Soli, tight, pulling at her fingers like she's trying to pull off invisible rings. 'As long as he doesn't open his mouth' – thinking it through – 'because he's got that ridiculous habit of being friendly, to everyone, as long as he *thinks*, yes.' Her voice rises in horror and yes, you repeat, yes. Because you've coached them all that they'll get into more trouble now by being honest than by making things up, but if anyone's not going to follow that advice it's your elder son, your shining boy. The *bugger*. So naughty that he ran away, and left his siblings behind. So selfish and unthinking; he'll get a slap for it, smart on the bum, when everything's right again, for what he's put you through. You won't forget this.

'Remind me,' Mouse is saying slowly, 'exactly *why* this might work?'

Soli takes a deep breath. 'Well, you know. His face always makes people . . . *like* him. And that has to be good. He bewitches them.'

Mouse says nothing. He hates that about his brother. Always wished he was an identical twin, wants the same face. 'Yeah,' he whispers now. 'People seem to . . . *adore* him, don't they?'

Your daughter mutters, God knows why, and gravely Mouse repeats, God knows why, but it's true, it's like he's spent his whole life seducing you and you always fall for it, you even steal him at night from his bed sometimes and just hold and hold him, kissing him, breathing him in, and now he's gone, lost, this has gone wrong, they're not meant to go off alone, they're stronger together than apart.

Often when I pray I wonder if I am not posting letters to a non-existent address.

∽ 68 ∽

Ten minutes. 'As long as he walks with confidence,' Soli says. 'He's got to walk straight down the middle of the corridors. He can't hug the walls. He has to walk like he belongs.'

'Actually,' Mouse says, 'I can't see the dude ever hugging a wall.'

Neither can you. Because Tidge is the St Bernard of the family, crashing through life with his big lollopy tongue and licking people adoringly, wherever he can, whoever he can get. He's not prepared for this, has no idea about fields that tremble for three days then stop.

WHY CAN'T YOU SEE HIM?

Nineteen minutes. He mustn't open his mouth in amazement; he has a habit of doing that. Close your mouth, my darling, you will him now, close your mouth, close your mouth.

You cannot bear this.

Anger now. Because he doesn't worry about pleasing others, he breezes through life, bugger the consequences, doesn't think. Mouse, on the other hand, is your thinker, your pleaser, and he has such a build-up of resentments because of it. Where is your sunny boy, where *is* he?

Twenty-eight minutes. Bewitch them, yes. Beauty is power and it's helped Tidge his entire life and it may help him now, please,

please yes. The unfairness of his brother's beauty has built up through the years like silt over Mouse's heart but you're all hoping now that Tidge's face is protecting him, because everyone's always gazing at him, ruffling his hair, transfixed; even though your heart is telling you this new world doesn't work like that any more, among those men out there who've lost their light hearts.

'*I* should have gone,' Mouse announces.

'If anyone was going to do this,' Soli says, 'it's him.'

She's right. Because he's the doer of the family. Your type always survive, you teased Mouse once; you lie low, you commentate, you watch. That makes me feel like a rat, he protested in response.

'I should have gone,' he now repeats, standing taller at that door than he's ever stood in his life.

'No,' Soli says fiercely, 'I'm not having you lost next.'

Only men of ability and virtue can give complete exhibition to the idea of sacrifice.

❧ 69 ❧

'He's gone to find the secret room controlling the hidden camera in the telly. I *know* him. He's gone to get Mum and Dad. He thinks they're . . . close. He wants to rescue them. He'll climb the crow's-nest of this city to search them out. I know him, he'll never stop.'

A white balloon scoots across the pavement and gusts into the air, tumbles like washing in a dryer, shrinks to a tadpole speck, a black dot, is nearly to heaven, gone.

Four little hands, splayed flat on the glass.

An enormous rush of love so fierce it hurts. When you were working in the lab you'd run, *run* up the driveway each night, needing to hold their hot squirmy bodies close, to smell them, bundle them up, all that bursting lovely life. How to bottle it? Oh, for that morning again when you were leaving for work and your lovely elder boy farewelled you at the door and called you back for another kiss and then another and instructed you gravely to buy a sandwich before you got to the office then kissed you again and you felt weighted with grace.

'He's petrified of being broken,' Mouse murmurs.

'I know.' We all do. Am I broken? he panics whenever he trips or knocks his head, quick, am I broken? And you have to check for blood and tell him it's not so bad because he's terrified of the sight. 'I have this vision of him out there somewhere, broken,'

Mouse says. 'And there's no one to help. No one to say, hey, it's nothing. Even though it is, I bet, I bet.'

Forty minutes. Your daughter's shaking. No words any more. Air taut.

Forty-nine. She's just yelled, 'I *hate* this, *hate* being grown up,' with her fingers clawed frozen at her head and the bones in her hands little rakes. 'I can't *do this* any more, can't live like this.' You stare in wonder, at yourself. At what she has turned into in this place.

You squeeze your eyes shut.

> *I tell you the truth,*
> *if you have faith as small as a mustard seed,*
> *you can say this to the mountain, 'Move from here to*
> *there,' and it will move.*

The key.

He's back.

Unfurl your heart.

Bursting into the room like a striker who's just clinched the World Cup (Mouse's love diminishes, a touch). 'You *won't* believe it.' Dropping to his knees, bursting with triumph.

'Mum?'

'Dad?'

'Well . . . *no* . . . but you wait.' He whips up his shirt and out tumble three bread rolls and a chicken leg and two cigarettes unlit which Soli promptly snatches.

'Not for another five years, mate,' and slips them into her pocket. 'Besides, you need a lighter.'

But Tidge pulls out a matchbox with a gleeful voilà and rattles it high and dances around the room in a delirious jogging dance, pumping his arms like a sprinter warming up.

'As silly as a wet hen,' Mouse observes, leaning against a wall.

'You next, dude, come on.' Tidge points at him.

'Excuse me. *I'll* decide who's next, thank you very much.' Soli snatches the matchbox. 'And I'll be twenty minutes. To the dot.' She glares at Tidge.

He dances his fingers up her tummy – 'Go on then, *go*' – cackling like he's drunk and flopping in a cartoon fall backwards onto the bed.

'And in a decade,' Mouse adds drily from his wall, 'we'll be wanting those cigarettes back.'

When a man speaks or acts with good intention
then happiness follows him like his shadow
that never leaves him.

∞ 71 ∞

So. Your two boys. Side by side now. Leaning against the wall. Tidge slinging an arm over his brother: 'Just try it, come on.' Mouse flinching him off. You sigh. It's always this. Your youngest wanting to stuff his brother's glee back inside him, like a sleeping bag into its sack, wanting to pull the toggle tight. You worry he'll grow into one of those men who slip through the cracks, who are lost. An adult who underlives and you dread that. He's always lagged with so much: eye contact, smiling, sport, making friends; has never had the rescue of a best mate. Old souls, so different, from the moment they were born. You sensed it. Tidge's theory is that all the waiting souls are hovering above the skin of the earth ready to slip into the parents they want, the flesh they need; that there's intention in their choice. 'I chose you to make you happy, Mummy,' Tidge explained, aged five. Mouse: 'I chose you for your toast.'

And when everything's going well for Tidge he grows bouncy and sleek and full of light. Which is now. And the one thing the twins have always had is the ability to second-guess each other but Tidge's breaking away here, going off on his own, thinking independently and they both know it. Tidge is shining as Mouse shrinks ever more glowery beside him, shining as his brother stands with his back against the wall and pushes him away. It's heartbreaking. They're growing up. It morphs into punching, Mouse attacking with a terrifying force and now they're rolling on the floor and kicking and hitting like two lion cubs and now the giggling comes, the change, just like that.

'Let's hide from her,' Tidge says suddenly.

Mouse looks at him sharp. Well, well, he can't say he disapproves. Perhaps his big brother's not completely lost to him yet.

Tidge surprises you sometimes with the shock of his nastiness. There's a side of him that doesn't know tenderness. He can't do a soft tickle, a loving stroke; yet complex little Mouse brims with sensual touch. The contradictions in all of them. They never stop wrong-footing you, there's always a next stage just as you think you've got them worked out.

Everyone goes about his business at the beginning of the day and sells his soul:
he either frees it, or causes it to perish.

∞ 72 ∞

Soli's back twenty minutes to the dot. Her eyes are sparkling, she's lit. 'Guys?'

An abandoned quiet.

'Hello?'

The voice of a little girl. She stares at the key in her hand. Shakes her head, quickly, as if she's trying to shake sense back into it. Runs to the bathroom, screeches aside the shower curtain. Runs out of the room moaning, 'No, no, come back.'

An explosion of giggling from under the bed.

'Get out.'

A furious, tear-brimmed voice.

She drags up Mouse, knows exactly whose fault this is. Her fingernails dig in hurting and deep. 'Don't you *ever* do that to me again, you . . . brat.' She shakes him viciously and he starts to yell but stops.

Because of something new in her.

Something exhausted, and old, and pushed to the brink.

Leave not a stain in thine honour.

∾ 73 ∾

It takes half an hour of apologies, half an hour of head massages and foot rubs to get to the crucial question: 'So what did you get?' Soli raises her eyebrows and retrieves a snowy white laundry sack she'd dropped by the door with a beautiful C embroidered upon it as golden as egg yolk. She pulls out a bottle of champagne.

'Ta da!'

'Hang on,' Mouse says dubiously, 'there's only half a glass in there. And no food.'

With a cheeky grin their sister lifts the bottle to her lips and luxuriantly swigs then she hands it across to her brothers and they drink too and she smiles like a cat with the warmest sill of sun and shakes out her hair and turns into someone looser and sillier, her eyes again lit, and your heart tightens to see it. Because she's got her old face back, all her freshness is suddenly in the room, her huge life force. She's so vivid-hearted, and it's been lost under all the strain, but now it's returned and you stand there watching with your fingertips pressed trembling at your mouth. At your effortlessly lovely girl back, blazing light.

Tidge finds his brother's hand, he's not shrugged off. 'It's Mum, dude,' he whispers.

'You look gorgeous, sis,' Mouse throws across and Soli swoops him into a cuddle which turns into a swirl.

'You next.' She chuckles affectionately, floating him, gently, to the ground. 'But only half an hour. Any longer and it's too stressful, for *everyone* left,' and she kicks Tidge playfully on the butt.

Is it true that our destiny is to turn into light itself?

∽ 74 ∾

But Mouse. Something's slunk away in him, like a dog with its tail between its legs.

'I'm happy just to stay here, guys. Unless . . . someone wants to come too.' His voice drops to a whisper. 'Maybe.' Oh, love. The nub of him. He's grown extremely comfortable with his boundary of 'no' that he's surrounded himself with over the years. Someone's always going to help him out and that thinking has built up like a shell now encasing him; fear has become a leash on his life. You've facilitated it. So of course he's happy right now to sit tight, safe, while everyone else figures out what to do next. But now this. A sister all pushy before him, his nerve-rash revving into life under her steely gaze, already claiming his cheeks, vining him, down, down, his neck, chest. It's a sorry sight.

'I want to go too.' His brother, loud into the shardy quiet.

'No. You're too obvious together.'

'I can't do it by myself,' Mouse whispers. No, he can't. And in that vast churning silence he rubs his arms where Soli yanked him from under the bed but her face does not change, she will win this. He stares at the speedy bruises on his skin, the yellow petals already on his flesh and Tidge's hand finds his shoulder, always there for him. Motl told them once that the difference with them is that there are yes-sayers and no-sayers and people who say yes are rewarded by the adventure they go on and people who say no are rewarded by their feeling of safety, and neither is better than the other, it's just the way they are. And they always have to respect the other's choice; they have to be their brother's protector and must never forget it.

'We *all* have to do this.' Soli, iron in her voice. The one who doesn't get weakness or maybe she does, too much. She spins Mouse around and propels him out.

'You were adopted. I think you should know, in case I don't come back.'

Soli's hands drop. 'I am not.' But a voice that believes it.

'Dad said so. I found the birth certificate in his drawer and I wasn't allowed to tell you.'

A new, electric quiet. Soli's paleness. Her mouth she forgot to shut. Mouse steps back. Pebbled now by the enormity of what he's unleashed. The taste of his meanness sour in his mouth.

'Get out,' Soli says finally.

'No, you weren't, I made it up.' Mouse laughs too loud. Trying to spool back the situation.

'Get out. We don't want you here. We don't need you. You're never any help.'

He frowns and rolls in his lips. Rooted, panicky, to the spot.

'And walk like you belong,' Soli says with a furious shove. 'Not that you belong anywhere.'

He had that coming. But there's the huge, glittery sting of it nonetheless. It's in his face.

Change, impermanence, is a characteristic of life.

❧ 75 ❧

The corridor. The door behind him. Just about to be firmly shut. Leaving Mouse stranded in the vast unknown. The boxer's back. His legs aren't working properly. It's like walking through thigh-high mud. 'Mummy,' he mouths, wildly looking around, 'Mummy?' You need to be with him, need this, he's so small, so young for this. You thump the wall in frustration.

And so it is. Thank God for that, thank God.

The corridor's empty. A hum like an engine room is somewhere close. Mouse's breathing ratchets up, his eyes are wide as he tries to work it out; perhaps there's a furnace or a lab for strange experiments or a child-sized oven warming up, and stopping at head height are rectangular, filthy cream tiles and above them are scrapes as if enormous crates have been pushed, protesting, into the building's dark heart. He gazes at the ceiling. Spaghetti lines of black piping run into the distance, ticking and gurgling and transporting goodness knows what. Water? Waste? Blood? He tries to spine his walk, to tall himself up, progressing slowly, so slowly down the corridor. Fire stairs, ahead. Can he do it? Can he climb them? He rubs his arms, feeling his sister's intent, still wears her finger marks. Up, up the steps, whimpering, barely managing this. To a heavy black door on the next level and he grabs a door handle and can't quite bring himself to turn it, to dare to see what's beyond, but, but . . .

He bends. Peers. A tiny, ripped-off piece of checked shirt, tied to the doorknob. So small it's hardly there. But it *is.*

His brother. A secret signal.
So. It must be all right. Someone's guiding him here.
Mouse smiles and turns the handle strong.

I am the door.

❦ 76 ❧

You gasp in shock. Well, well.

So *this* is B's world that he never talks about. Of course not. It would never fit the image of the renegade guerrilla hero in his biker boots, the principled fighter who sleeps on potato crates. 'Oh, my God,' Mouse whispers as he gazes through the door. 'Oh, my God.'

A cavernous hall of loveliness, too much loveliness in a country so smashed. Marble, gleaming mirrors, shine. A colour scheme of black and silver and cream. Light streaming through a glass dome in enormous bands like highways for angels, highways to up and out. Your boy grips the door handle, the last bit of reality from his other, room-boxed life. He shuts the door and leans against the tiles. Can't step out into this, can't believe it's real, can't ever walk normally into such an audacious place. How on earth did they manage such a secret? Party so ebulliently while ranting against everything this room represents.

Again Mouse opens the door, can't help it. The handle on the other side is a golden dolphin and looped on its jaunty tail is another of Tidge's strips. He smiles. Of course his brother drank this up. He glances at orchids cascading in pale waterfalls from vases as tall as toddlers, at chairs with carved eagles' heads on velvet arms, at chandeliers an umbrella span across, at a pianist's sad back among fat silver teapots and women with hard faces in high heels and red lipstick. The new regime was never meant to be this. It shrilled that it was fighting the voraciousness of the previous political caste, people that it spat had perfected the art of denying themselves nothing, who were obscenely immoral, excessive, corrupt. They were going to create a nobler, fairer, *corrected* way of life. Which was never this.

And B is embedded within it.

And where is Motl in all this? He said he knew his friend so well, like a son. Did he have any idea of this place? Any idea where his children might end up?

Mouse can't walk out into it, he's not brave enough. But there'll be his sister's knowing nod if he returns empty-handed; you all know she's expecting failure. He lifts his chin, takes a deep, firming breath, and steps out. You smile in disbelief.

When thou hast enough, remember the time of hunger.

∽ 77 ∾

A white marble staircase curves like a seashell up to the floors above, up to a secretive quiet. Tidge went there, of course. It's where his food came from, people leave uneaten food in hotel corridors, yes, but how did he get up?

A lift. Dead ahead. An old iron cage for a door that opens as if reading his thoughts. A uniformed lift-operator bows her head, all enquiring eyebrows and chuff. Your son nods in return with a wan grin not quite there on his face. The woman twinkles a smile and sweeps her hand across the showroom of her tiny space. And a lift-operator, good grief, it's like seeing a video player or a cassette. Motl would love it so much. He'd settle on her velvet bench and travel up and down, up and down, all cackly with delight. Your son holds high his hand firmly in farewell. Shuts his door. So not good at this. He climbs the stairs and skips the first floor and opens the fire door with a 2 on it.

'Lost?' The lift lady chuckles, dead ahead.

'No,' Mouse grumps. Annoyed that he's been second-guessed.

A stand-off. She's not leaving. Her face has so much memory in it. And it's been such a long time since Mouse has seen anyone elderly and he steps forward without realising, as if suddenly transfixed by the idea of her house, all those early childhood smells from visits to Granny, stillness and airless rooms and smothery, powdery cuddles and flannellette sheets.

'Why are you wandering about all alone, young man? Are you lost? Can I help?'

'What's your name?' he deflects.

'Jude Pickering the Third,' she announces with a smile. 'And don't you forget.'

He smiles and it's like sun breaking through cloud. The woman closes the lift door with fingers as yellow and as worn as old newspapers and whispers that there's an old service lift if he'd prefer, pointing with a blue-roped hand to a door down the corridor covered in wallpaper.

'Hardly anyone uses it because it's so slow. But you might just enjoy it, I think.'

Then she's gone. Her knowing twinkle the last thing left.

And you are not afraid. She's one of you, you're sure of it. Perhaps, just perhaps, B is on track. And there are people looking out for them, and they'll be all right.

Miss not the discourse of the elders.

∞ 78 ∞

And now your little boy. Standing in that hotel corridor with an enormous warmth filling him up. Because he *did* it – he walked out of that terrifying door of his room into the vast unknown. By himself. And it worked. He found kindness and his father's always going on about that. It's attached to Motl's favourite word, *empathy*; he says that kindness requires empathy which requires imagination and many people in this world have it, many unexpected people, you just have to give them the chance and this lift lady has demonstrated it; she put herself into your son's shoes and imagined what it must be like. And tried to help. And your boy can't stop grinning with the stun of it. He's standing here, all changed, one huge streak of grin, and then he's off.

And for no reason I start skipping like a child.

⤳ 79 ⤳

Now a tray. Any food he can get. Time's running out. The corridor feels like a house where everyone has to speak in whispers, where someone's died and all the children must be quiet. Behind a door Mouse can hear a TV's chattery daytime hum and he scuttles away and turns a corner and there's a lone tray at the end. Quick. Nothing on it but some half-eaten pasta and a cold pot of tea and a dreg of milk that's drained in a gulp. The bowl of pasta's grabbed, it'll have to do. He runs back to the wallpapered door and plunges through it.

A scuffed landing. Lit by a light bulb as weak as sickness. A tiny room full of towels. Shampoos. Soaps. He fills his pockets with as many toiletries as he can get then presses the lift button, praying that no one else is in it, and watches the numbers rise steadily up, up, from B, basement, and his throat tightens, ready to run if he must. The door opens.

Empty. Thank goodness.

Empty all the shuddery way down.

Mouse slams back against the lift wall with relief.

That Miss Jude Pickering the Third was right. He so much prefers it like this. It's as if she's been briefed.

HEY, it's like this invisible network of watching around us. Good people, out there. Everywhere. Keeping us safe. Thanks.

Your skin prickles up.

He who formerly was thoughtless
and afterwards cultivates awareness
brightens up the world like the moon when free of clouds.

❦ 80 ❦

Some people are really like, still there, when they die. I mean their presence. The bigness of their life force. It's like the air is stamped with them. You can feel it. Their, I dunno, lingering. You'd think the logical place for them would be asleep underground but no way, they're anywhere but that. It's like they're hanging on for a bit. Then they're gone. Just like that. They suddenly move on.

<u>Hence the command, 'Listen in silence,' and be silent: since you have not become the tongue of God, be ears.</u>

❧ 81 ❧

The back end of the night. A glary glee in each of them. Soli draws the curtains. They need the pitch dark, as dark as they can get. Tiny pinpricks of wily light shine through the moth-holes but it's fine, black enough. For the fireworks!

And so here they all are, your three shining children, peeling off their piled-on clothes which crackle and flare in the dry air and they're all shrieking at each fresh spark-shower that stands their freshly washed hair on stilty end, your daughter's the most, and they're doing it over and over until the sparks grow less and stop. Their little world in this room is shining right up now and they're drunk with the joy of it. Tidge, especially, has come over all silly tonight, anything's setting him off. His sister singing into the champagne bottle, her ravenous belly button that swallows fingers to the second knuckle, everyone's horizontal hair, the way it smells different on each one of them even though they're all using the same shampoo. 'Wicked,' he announces as he buries his nose into any head he can get and his siblings keep pushing him off but back he comes and back, puppy-persistent, collapsing them into giggles until their sides ache and they can hardly stand, hardly talk. Exuberance is beauty, oh yes, and there's such a cram of beauty in this room tonight, a halo of joy. Binding them, soothing them, mending them.

It is love. It is relief.

Their space is sanctified by it, and you are at peace.

*And in the time of their visitation they shall shine
and run to and fro like sparks among the stubble.*

∽ 82 ∾

Now the tired is leaking into each of them and one by one they wind down and grow quiet and stop. Your daughter's hand is resting lightly on Tidge's jutting hip and it's not shrugged off. Her forehead's smooth, something within her has passed. Tidge sleeps with his arms spread wide and Mouse, the last awake, takes out his notebook, chuckling in wonder at his brother's trust, still; that magnificent and persistent belief that everything will be all right. Mouse wants it so much. The buoyancy of it, the release.

'I've grown into religion,' Motl declared towards the end. 'And you know, Mrs, I'm not sure now that humans can ever, as a species, completely move beyond it. Maybe we're programmed always to create a spiritual world around us.'

'Excuse me, Mr, but I happen to think *precisely* the opposite. Humanity's growing out of it, my lovely addled love. It's evolution. Religious people say they're inspired by faith and certainty – but that puts them in direct conflict with science. And science is winning.'

'Certainty is dangerous in both science and religion, my lovely addled love. Each one, ultimately, is about uncertainty. In mystery lies the sublime. There are things that can be told and things that will never be told, you have to accept that.'

'Yeah yeah, yada yada.'

'Can goodness evolve, do you think?'

'No. I despair of the world. Well, *men.*' You glared and poked him playfully in the ribs. 'Predation, not parity, is nature's organising principle. We prey on others. We always have, always will. We thieve land and lives because that's nature. We're animals, human animals, the ugliest of the lot. And now I'm knackered. Nigh-night.'

> *As soon as you hold the view that this is 'true',*
> *friction arises;*
> *because the opposite view must then be*
> *termed 'false'.*

❧ 83 ❧

Deep in this long dark all Mouse's worry is crowding back. He's tried falling into sleep on his rocky ledge of fret but tosses and turns.

Okay. Slip into Tidge's thinking. Try. Come ON. That we're being looked after. That we don't have to worry because someone else is doing it for us. Shed the fear. Let it go.

His eyes are closing. He's floating, smiling. He wakes.

WOW. Dreaming just then of Salt Cottage. Snow was coating it. Protecting it under a white sheet of forgetting. Hiding it away so that it's waiting there patiently just for us, silent and enchanted. Our paradise lost! Dad's final secret was to kick our football into a far corner of the garden so it'll always be there for us, untouched, except by the wind. That football is STILL THERE. I'm SURE. Waiting silently for the five of us to get back. Yippeee!!

You smile. Kick-about was the only sport you ever managed as a family. You'd all scramble out on one of those insanely fresh, wind-whipped days and whoop with laughter when you'd score a miraculous goal and topple onto your back under the beautiful tall sky with your arms spread wide, giggling madly, unable to stop. At the mummy side of you dissolving, at becoming someone else. The woman you once were, you guess.

154

And you're smiling now as little knotted Mouse drifts off into contented sleep, beside his brother, and you press close to his dreaming blood and climb on a black wing higher and higher over the city with the world below you shrinking to a web of lights, shrinking to darkness, going, going, gone. You shut your eyes, you are safe, you are safe, and you all fall into a deep sleep with the gift of that.

Do not surrender your loneliness so quickly.
Let it cut more deep. Let it ferment and season you.

∽ 84 ∾

Tidge wakes late in the morning within a net of drowsiness. His brother's ankle is heavy over his. He feels scrubbed by the events of yesterday. There's promise in the new day's cleanness. He sits up and listens. Bells outside are trying to pull the world to their god. The sound is like the bleat of a lamb in a frosted field, bleakly alone. It shuts off abruptly as if silenced by force.

> *They will not cease to war against you until they turn you from your religion.*

❧ 85 ❧

What you crave: a place with melodramatic skies again. Where the silence hums, where your eye rests. A God-charged landscape. The grace of that. What you want to tell Motl: that you have come to something of an understanding of a spirituality beyond religion; a stirring within, a stillness, a strength; and you suspect that men have harnessed the shock of that over the centuries for their own, belligerent, use. To control. Divide. Belittle. Subjugate women. Grasp. All their roaring words, in all their roaring books. You have found it in the land and you have found it in the aftermath of giving birth but you have not found it in his volumes that he left you, all his volumes, written by all those men, and so there is no place for you in any of those religions. Everyone creates it for themselves, oh yes. Perhaps he also came to that conclusion but you never allowed him the concession of an honest discussion, you just ridiculed his beliefs as unthinking and embarrassing and duped. He, in turn, thought you were beyond reach, stranded behind your impenetrable wall of judgement, husked.

Churches destroy the mystery of God.

86

Tidge. Oh Tidge. Not *again*. Late from another expedition. 'Me first, can I?' he'd begged his siblings.

Soli had ruffled his hair and laughed – 'Go on, off you go' – shooing out his jogging dance of impatience complete with forehead glued to the door, and snatching the key back.

But now. He *knew* the timekeeping rule. You all trusted him to keep to it. You're furious with him. Soli's bitten down every one of her nails. Two are bleeding. Mouse says he's got a funny feeling. His eyes are afraid. Soli draws in a trembling breath. Pulls her ponytail tight. Says she's going out and hauling her brother back, by the earlobe if she must. She'll have to go over the entire building – the lobby, basement, roof – because you all know Tidge is a lookaholic and his curiosity is careless and vast; she crouches in front of Mouse and tells him to lock the door and not to mention Mum and Dad to a soul, no matter what.

'We can't trust *anyone*, all right?'

'I'm the cynic of the family, remember. The survivor. It's the other one we have to worry about.'

His sister doesn't laugh.

The Lord is with thee, though mighty man of valour.

✂ 87 ✂

Mouse grazes stillness. The wind outside slicks a piece of paper around a man's leg. The breeze seems very far away. He flops on the mattress and spreads his limbs into a starfish. Writes.

A bed finally to myself. Lonely, and I wasn't expecting that.

Standing now, back against the door. So small, unsure, lost. He turns. He slips the key into the lock, takes it out, holds it to his lips. Not wanting to go out by himself, must. All briared up; bound by terror of what's gone wrong and why aren't they back; bound by terror of himself. He wailed to you once he wasn't good at being alive and how come Tidge was? 'Come on,' he now revs himself up, 'for God's sake just *go*.'

If you want others to be happy, practise compassion.
If you want to be happy, practise compassion.

❧ 88 ❧

Mouse locks the door from the outside and just as he slips the key into his pocket his two siblings bolt down the corridor. *Safe.* Gloriously in one piece and no blood, nothing broken; everything, miraculously, all right. You're cracked like an egg into runniness and relief. The three of them burst into the room. Your two eldest are holding hands, won't let go, can't, as if it's impossible to stop touching now that contact's been made and their faces are incredulous because they've made it, they're safe.

'You little monkey.' Soli attacks Tidge with tickles on the bed. 'You absolute little monkey. You are *so* dead, mate.'

He was starving. Of course. And he had a plan. He'd set out early because there'd be breakfast trays then and possibly, even, jam toast. He'd go to the top floor because the people up there would be richer and the women more afraid of getting fat, so more things would be left. Tidge let himself out of the room with its fidgety sky. Didn't tell his sister because she'd just say no in her mother voice and didn't tell his brother because nothing impresses him much. He climbed the fire stairs to a door with a six. A peek was promising. It felt like a very expensive shop that hardly anyone ever goes into. Someone almost saw him, a security guard, but he'd forgotten to place a bet so he told his friend the other guard who wanted a bet too and down they both went in the lift. And out Tidge stepped. His feet sank into carpet like it wanted to eat them but there was a tray at the end of the corridor and just as Tidge was plucking a raspberry from a pancake a voice behind him yelled out. He jumped. Spun, with a thudding heart.

It was a boy. A boy! A potential friend.

'How did you get here?'

Tidge couldn't speak, think.

'Do . . . you . . . understand?'

'Yes,' your boy squeaked. 'I got lost.'

'Are you a guest?'

'Uh-huh,' he said. Then quickly asked a pressing question: 'Marvel or D.C. heroes?'

'D.C., what do you expect?'

'Snap! Me too. Any comics?'

'Ah, like, yeah. And maybe, even, a game or two.'

Tidge sucked in his breath in ecstasy. 'Can I play?'

The boy sighed.

And in that adult response Tidge got the feeling the new person had rarely had a friend in his life. It was something about the shirt buttoned up to the neck and the careful face and the eyes shifting away from him, not looking at him straight. He willed him to say yes.

'Okay,' the boy said finally, warily. 'But we'll have to be quick. My dad doesn't allow visitors.'

Your son laughed and slung his arm over the shoulders of his brand-new best mate. He never sees the colour of skin, never hears an accent, never notices difference; to him it's always just a kid, a new playmate. And he noted as they walked down the corridor that this new boy walked differently. Without fear. Like he belonged.

So your little man had a go at walking like that. And back in their room gleefully demonstrated.

Just the art of being kind is all the sad world needs.

∽ 89 ∽

But Soli. Furious with herself because she'd been entrusted with her brothers' safety and it was all going pear-shaped; taking enormous risks to get everything back right. She poked her head into restaurants and listened in at doors. Finally, one floor left, the sixth. On the handle of its fire door was a ribbon of shirt. She held it to her lips shaking with relief. Heard, suddenly, her brother's shriek. Her heart jolted, she couldn't read it, joy or alarm? She tried the door where it came from. Locked. She'd have to knock. Agony. This was becoming too hard, her parents were expecting too much; she hesitated, closed her eyes, breathed deep: then, as if plunging into a very cold pool, held her breath and rapped. Attagirl.

A careful boy. Reddening. Soli also. Her wayward brother barging between them.

'We've been playing computer games – D.C. heroes – and I won, sis, I *won*.'

'Well, just.'

'*Who* is this?' A barely suppressed explosion in Soli's voice.

'Pin. My friend. Isn't that a cool name? And he's got—'

'Where are your mum and dad, Pin?'

'My father's out.'

'Well, I think we'll keep this little play date to ourselves. And *you*, young man' – she looked severely at her brother – 'it's time we went.'

'But we're right in the middle of—'

'*Right* now.'

A tense stand-off. Your son wasn't budging. He'd found a new mate, he wasn't going to give him up; he'd found a new life, a possible way out.

'Mum's downstairs. Waiting.'

Tidge gasped. He believed it, for a second, it was in his face.

Soli's heart hurt to see it. But she had him, in that moment he was caught. She grabbed his hand and yanked.

By rousing himself, by thoughtfulness, by self-discipline,
the wise man can make for himself an island
which no flood can overwhelm.

❧ 90 ❧

Tidge is now sitting next to his sister, their backs against the cupboard. They're singing 'Let's go fly a kite, up to the highest heights'. Mouse is inside, writing.

Good grief. My brother is impersonating my sister. The two of them are singing together. My WORST nightmare. It has become reality. I have to get out.

Soli's conducting using B's key held high in the air. Mouse eventually puts down his notebook and joins them to steer them into tune. So. Here they all are. Singing away like there's no tomorrow, singing away as if to lock laughter and light forever in their hearts. Because once again they made it, they're safe and they're becoming good at it. Mouse gives up eventually and lets the two of them veer off course.

A sharp knock.

'Hello? Anyone in there?'

The new boy's followed them. He pokes his head around the door. Steps inside.

They're found out. Your blood runs cold. You feel disembodied, floating; the door is unlocked; in the relief of being safe everyone forgot, or they were going to do it next or they've become careless or whatever, they're found out. Caught. Tidge and Soli leap up, glee wiped. Mouse stays in the cupboard, trapped.

'Hey, guys, what's up?' the boy says mildly.

Silence, wire-taut. You will your daughter to do the talking. Will your son to stay quiet.

'We found this place,' Soli says carefully, 'we were just . . . mucking about.'

'I don't think so.' Like a grown-up is already underneath.

'All right,' Soli says. Her frantic thinking. 'We're hiding.' She's walking across thin ice; any moment it could break, like a pistol shot; you shut your eyes, will her safe; will this boy from the other side gone, gone from their tender lives. 'Our parents are away. We got in from the street. If we're turned in' – her voice goes very small – 'I don't know what will happen to us.' Silence. The ice is creaking, bowing, Mouse pumps his hands in terror, little sickles of blood appear in his palms, from his nails, tiny scythes.

'Where are you from?' The voice cold. You do not like him, cannot detect warmth.

'The north,' Soli says precisely as Tidge leaps in with 'The west.'

A new silence. Grubby and wrong.

'Are you street kids?'

No one answers.

'Your parents have been disappeared, haven't they?'

Mouse rams a hand at his mouth to stop a sob because it's been said, finally, after so many nights of wondering and not daring to say, to speculate, talk it out because it can't be that, anything but, and now the tears come; no, no, he mouths and *nooooo* Tidge yells with all the force of his brother's heart. Because if you've been disappeared you're never coming back, they're alone, and they'll never know what happened and their lives will be spent trying to work it out and they couldn't bear it, they need a compass of certainty to go on with this.

'They're away. On business. For a month.' Soli speaks calmly but you sense the will in her to even out her voice. 'We ran

165

away. From our uncle. He was looking after us. We don't like him. We thought a hotel might be a good place to get food. And be . . . safe.' She says that word soft like it is lit by a candle and reaches across to her little brother and draws him in tight. 'That's all we want.'

'Hrumph,' the intruder says as if he doesn't believe any of it, one bit.

In the name of God, the compassionate, the merciful.

91

'Maybe we should keep him,' Tidge says, moving towards the door with the key now in his hand. 'You know, like a hostage.'

'You can't,' Mouse responds quick from the cupboard.

'Who's that?' The boy spins.

'It creates more problems than it solves.' Mouse steps out, holding up a hand in warning to his brother. 'Hi. Good to meet you.' Warily Pin allows his palm to be shaken. Mouse encloses the stranger's fingers warmly, hugely, in a double clasp, just like his father often does in greeting.

Pin looks at one boy then the other and back again.

'Twins,' Mouse explains.

'So you get two of us for the price of one,' Tidge says.

'Believe me, I'm more of a bargain than he is,' Mouse adds drily.

A smile. Not a laugh but a smile. It's a start. A fragile one. But everyone's heart is thudding. Everyone's.

They strive after violence on the earth.

❦ 92 ❦

He leans against the wall with his arms crossed. A sizzly new presence in their midst. And it's in your blood to despise them. Fear them. Dismiss them. Want them gone from your land and your life. You do not like their difference, their smell, language, pushiness, how they treat their women, how they disregard life. And now the banality of what he could so easily do. To the things most precious to you.

He takes in the scattered clothes, the empty trolley, the doll and the book. Looking and looking, trying to work your kids out, what they're doing in this place. The three of them breathe tremulous, light, waiting for his response.

'Hell,' he declares finally. Like it's the best lawn for football in the street.

'We know.' Tidge smiles in enormous relief.

'So, like, what are you going to do next?'

Your children are blank.

'We want to go home,' Mouse says finally. 'We're going to make it, too, you know.' A firm, adult voice that stands you tall.

But Soli. Standing by the door. Shaking. You can tell by her hands, they won't be still. You know her. She can't see any good in this and blames herself, she should have kept a tighter rein on those slippery boys; a runaway locomotive has been set in motion here and she's not sure now it can ever be stopped; nothing's under control and at any moment B might come back and be dragged into this mess and Mum and Dad too; they could all be compromised and everything broken, smashed. Because they disobeyed B. They went out. Everything sprang from that.

Tidge has no idea. He puts his arm around his new friend and coaxes him to the curtains, for a swing. 'Come on.' He laughs. 'You first!'

This great pull in us to connect.

∞ 93 ∞

As soon as Pin's gone Mouse grabs the doll from the sill and holds him to his chest and blurts defensively in one breath, 'Dad says we should always try to hold out a hand, to anyone, no matter what, to increase the amount of kindness in the world and it's always worth the effort and it may, actually, help, all right?' He gulps a breath. 'So don't get cross.'

A long quiet. Soli says okay. She sits down carefully on the bed as if she's very old and tired and her body won't work properly any more. She says she'd like Tidge to tell her everything he knows about this new friend. '*Everything*,' and there is viciousness in that word. Tidge sits beside her. Begins.

Right. Well. It couldn't be much worse.

Pin's father is cemented into the heart of the government. He works for the Interior Office.

'What's that?' Tidge asks.

'Jails, detention, stuff like that,' Soli replies. 'The Official Truth Commission. The Department for Historical Clarification. All those places where people get taken away and never come back.'

Mouse shrinks into a curl on the bed. Tidge talks on. Pin is now staying in this place for protection because his old house is a target and his father has a complicated past, he was a doctor but now he's not.

Ah yes, yes, you know of him. A man obsessed by violence, an extreme but not uncommon example of clinicide. Doctors who kill. God. Could it be any worse? One of that esteemed coterie of medical practitioners involved in their country's murderous pasts. His historical colleagues: Jean-Paul Marat, Mengele, Papa Doc Duvalier, Radovan Karadzic and, cult notwithstanding, Che Guevara. And what, exactly, attracted them to the profession in the first place? The power over life or death? This man, early on, was notoriously involved in the slaughter of twelve men, in a single room, with sledgehammers. And what, precisely, is the thought behind that? You whimper as your son talks, you whimper, cannot stop.

Pin's been kidnapped before, abduction's now rampant in your country and he's a bargaining chip and he spends all his time quarantined as a consequence. 'He's like this hidden-away prince,' Tidge says, eyes wide. His father has an intractable hatred of people like us; Pin, apparently, does not. 'And you know what? He could be a way out!' He says excitedly.

Mouse shoots bolt upright. His response is vicious and fast. 'Yes. We want our home and our parents back, but with *his* help? I don't think so. We can never trust someone like that. The grown-up *must* have leaked into him. He *must* have been stained by the hate.'

But Tidge ambles on. Pin has promised to keep the secret of their hiding place so long as he can muck around with them, whenever he wants; he's worked it out, he's telling his guards he's off for a swim, every day, and he's so excited about having brand-new people, *kids*, at last, in his life.

'Those people kill people like us,' Mouse says.

'But we kill them,' Tidge responds, matter-of-fact. 'We might as well trust him, dude, it's in his face. It's a face that's incapable of—'

'Stop,' Mouse cries, covering his ears. 'Stop, you idiot, stop.'

Between us and you there is a great gulf fixed.

∽ 94 ∽

'You're not *thinking*.' Mouse, later, shouting to his brother. Stabbing his temples with his index fingers. 'If we're taken away this is all your fault, all right? You didn't *have* to play those stupid super-hero games. And remember, Tidge, you're a boy, just like me. And we're not going to be in a group that's walking down the street. They'll be separating us. They'll be taking us away to a field that trembles for three days and then stops. You. And me. And you know what? You'll have brought it all on yourself. We can all blame you for that, no one else. Thanks, mate. Thanks a lot.' Mouse stops, clamping his hand at his mouth at the ugliness that's come out. Too late.

His brother's as white as flour, running to the bathroom, slamming the door shut like he's never slammed a door in his life.

A vibrating stillness.

The leaving of the light.

He shall return no more to his house,
neither shall his place know him any more.

172

❧ 95 ❧

So. Here they are. The three of them, found out. Your youngest child curled by the bathroom door, horrified at the too-quick words that blurted from his mouth. His brother inside, too quiet. Your daughter in a tight zigzag on the bed. Mouse can't stop staring at the door, silently beseeching his brother to emerge out. He's never been like this. God knows what's ahead. There's no map any more, their future can't be read.

Dad said we have to remember that the family is the basic unit of society. NOT a person acting alone. The mantra, the mantra. 'That we're stronger TOGETHER than apart.' And we have to do WHATEVER IT TAKES to keep together. He looked at me specially when he said this. WHY can't I keep my mouth shut? I NEVER learn. Okay. It's official. I should never have been born. I should not be on this planet mucking everything up. I'm NO USE. All right?

Achingly you want to break through the membrane of their world; achingly you want to scoop them up, your three lone chicks, tumbled, tumbled from their nest.

He that diggeth a pit shall fall into it.

∞ 96 ∞

Midnight. Mouse thudding into Soli's warmth in the dark, curving round her back and clinging on, mutual hot-water bottles in the clustering cold. It is as if the chill wants to slip straight through them tonight, into their bones, to curl up and nest. Tidge hasn't emerged from the bathroom. He's locked himself in, hasn't said a peep. His brother's in the bed vividly awake. Hating who he is. All the scatter-gun words that come out.

Okay, it's official, Dad. THE RETREAT FROM WONDER. I'm sorry. It's gone. Kaput.

Motl dreaded it would ever come to this. Their world glooming down like a fish tank clouding over with a lack of light. Hope lost.

The air is thin here. Breathing is hard. And sleeping. It's like being stranded up a rocky mountain in some high altitude of despair and you can't go forward or back. How much longer will we be here? Where is G? We can't leave, even though we should. Can't have him returning to an empty room and reporting to Mum and Dad that we've vanished and the thread to them is cut. And we're out in the world somewhere, lost.

174

No stars tonight. The orange glow from the street lights has bled them away. You never see stars in this place. Your city nieces told you once that they only happen in movies, and how you laughed at the time, at what their world had become. That was before your nieces went. 'They've gone to another country,' you'd say abruptly, to the endless enquiries, 'they got out, before it's too late,' and then you'd glance across at Motl with something like hate. You couldn't bear to read their letters in the end, their missives from exile shouting of a new life.

You need a real sky tonight. Something dark and weighty and rich, a sky you can read not this weak orange glow.

It feels like the world is shutting down. That one by one all the rooms are being locked up and the sheets thrown over furniture and the lights turned off.

Your Soli's crying. She hardly ever cries; it's a shock. She's doing it quietly pretending she isn't. Her whole body's shuddering in tiny spasms as she tries to hold it in but can't. Mouse looks at her in panic. Glances across at the bathroom. Each sob is a little hook into your heart. Eventually your little boy curls around his sister and tucks his hand firmly under her arm and soothes, 'Sssh, it's all right, sssh.'

Do the dead help? IS ANYONE OUT THERE?

Where is your man? Where? You have no sense of him, no certainty. Is he with B, are they planning a rescue, is he lost, fighting this, fired up? The unknowing is a black hole of grief. You shut your eyes, he's holding you again in sleep, his arm slinging around your waist in a belt of warmth. He's scraping back your hair as you're crouching over the toilet bowl and vomiting in the first flush of pregnancy, he's putting his head to your stomach and telling his tadpole child not to make Mummy sick. He taught you that good sex is a spiritual experience and the best sex profound, he taught you that at the height of ecstasy you're taken to another place and that place is above all transcendent, God's gift perhaps, his lure, his little chuckle. Because of course from sex comes that most magnificent decision in all of life: to create it. Which together you did. Three times, with the most solemn and sanctified intent.

> *Nature herself has imprinted on the minds of all*
> *the idea of God.*

✂ 97 ✂

When Mouse wakes, the world seems different. The light is bright, accusing; it's the latest he's slept in this place. Soli is perky on the end of the bed. The old book is on her lap. Her hands are flat like a pharaoh's upon it. She's waiting for her boys. They're side by side, lover close. Tidge crawled beside his brother in the early morning and a smile fills Mouse up when he realises. 'Wake him,' Soli now instructs. Mouse shakes him and he makes a whiny noise and turns over with a hrumph and puts the blanket over his head; it's a manoeuvre perfected through years of practice; he's still asleep. Mouse tugs. Tidge sits bolt upright. Soli takes a tiny key from her pocket and slips it into the book's padlock. It springs open gratefully at her touch. She lifts the cover. Both boys lean. Gasp.

It's not a book at all. It's a box.

Its golden sides are carved to resemble paper. The front cover is a lid and inside is a multitude of tiny bundles packed tight. Gently, reverently, your daughter lifts out each little shroud and places them in a forensic line upon the bed. 'It's a memory box,' she whispers. 'From Mum.' She looks at them both. 'For all of us.'

The boys stare, open-mouthed, in wonder. And as their sister unwraps each familiar item from their Salt Cottage life you wonder if they realise that you have packed love itself into this box, just like you used to years ago, with their school lunches; among the sandwiches and fruit you'd always slip little treats:

a novelty pencil or a speckled feather, a beautifully shaped stone or a spotted egg. Your throat tightens as you watch. Can they feel the fierceness of your love in each object? Can they ever know it?

'She's everywhere,' Tidge whispers.

'But where we know,' Mouse adds quiet.

You are so in love with life.

It is the spirit that quickeneth.

❧ 98 ❧

THE MEMORY BOX
A List by Heart

1: Tiny shells from our beach. A scattering of frail bleached
thumbnails that smell of home.

*2: A drawing from when I was five of all of us with our two
pets, Bucket, the three legged dog, and Biscweet the cat
addicted to dad's lap.* The twitcher who burned his tail in
the toaster. *My sister married Bucket once but divorced him
when he sicked on her bed (HA HA). That picture was always
on our fridge, whatever fridge we had, in whatever home.* The
last place, Salt Cottage, a kitchen anointed by the sun.

*3: Mum's dangly earrings like teardrops. Mum has lots of
earrings but she's only packed these ones.* Your only screw-
ons, your best.

*4: An empty oyster shell. It's for me me me, no one else! I ate
an oyster once and laughed and laughed. 'Hey, Mum, I
swallowed the sea!'* And was always pestering you for more.

5: A pot of Vicks VapoRub. They take it in turns to sniff deep.
*It plunges me back instantly to snuffly nights of rain on the
roof and flat lemonade and honey toast.* Yes, yes.

6: A scrap of the busy jumpy wallpaper in our bedroom with the cowboys and horses on it. Who'd sleep with that, I always moan (sorry, Mum). What were you thinking? No wonder he's neurotic, it's the wallpaper's fault.

7: Mum's little old manicure set. The powder in its compact is worn to a pale hardness. *It smells of Granny, of kissing her cheek.* For your girl and she knows it.

8: A postcard from Mum's favourite artist, Rothko. It's always on the fridge too. She says there was a time long ago in our country when art and beauty and calm not only existed but were celebrated. That time will come back. The world swings, regenerates, forgets.

9: Instructions from Dad's grumpy typewriter he refuses to toss in spite of its disobedient E.

```
        — NOTES FOR THE LITTLE MONKEYS —

BEd for twins by 9 and thEy MUST do a wEE
bEforEhand. No ghost storiEs for TidgE bEcausE
hE'll havE bad drEams. (HE bEliEvEs EVERYTHING.)
ChEck regularly for nits Esp. if somEonE is
scratching thEir hEad Esp. around thE Ears and
thE back of thE nEck. Gritchy usually mEans slEEp.
MousE will always gEt sickEr than TidgE EvEn though
thEy usually gEt thE samE thinG. TEEth brushEd
morning and night. DO NOT GROW DULL. DO NOT UNDER-
LIVE. FIND THE BEAUTY IN EVERYTHING. DO NOT LOSE
YOUR SHINING SPIRITS. YOU MAKE US LAUGH SO MUCH.
WE LOVE YOU FOR THAT.
```

I hold the paper over my face and breathe in the greed of Mum's love. Can just picture her typing away at this. She'd always do it so elegantly. A conductor not of music but of words.

And now this, your last work, your symphony of the splayed heart. Behind his typewritten sheet is a scrap of kitchen towel with your scrawl that gets worse over the years.

Soli's laugh
Tidge's cough
Mouse's hand

He frowns, confused, then smiles.

Of course. These things aren't ours but our parents'. The laugh and left-handedness Mum's. The cough Dad's. He holds the sheet to the light. *The handwriting's dug deep. Mum stabbed the end of the pen viciously into her chest to get it working. Time must have been short.* You were stressed. The pen didn't properly work. The watcher observes well.

10: *A dried-out leaf. Soli says if it's crushed the smell will take us back to Salt Cottage.* He holds it flat in his palm then closes his fingers over it, hovering a crushing, wanting home so much. Gently she takes it from him. 'Not now, not yet.'

11: *An envelope with some feathery mats of my baby hair and another with Tidge's. Wow. We've got completely different colours now.* The first letters of their names identify which is which. *Dad shaved his head when we were six months old because our hair had refused to grow and he did it out of solidarity.* But he was enormously relieved when at fourteen months, at last, their hair began to sprout, and he could have his back.

12: *The last teacup, that one with the red spots, that used to hold Mum's champagne when she told her stories.* And now he weeps.

13: *A key. Old-fashioned. Too big.*

'Is that our house key?' Tidge asks.

'Yes,' his sister replies then hastily adds, 'no, perhaps,' as if she's imagining her little brother making a dash for home that very second, clutching the key like there's no tomorrow left. She begins packing each item back. 'Maybe this wasn't such a good idea . . .'

14: *A photo of a football on a lawn. It could be any ball, any lawn, but we all know it.* He holds it tight and his sister eventually stops her tugging and whispers, 'Have it, go on.' She hands the key to his brother. 'Mum said to imagine that this opens whatever we want. Keep it safe. For all of us.'

'What about you?' Mouse protests. 'What have you got?'

'Nothing. I don't need—'

'You have to have *something*.'

Soli sighs. Looks in the box. Plucks out the paper towel with your writing gouged deep.

A blanket of quiet, a blanket of absolute quiet.

<u>*That is happiness:*</u>
<u>*to be dissolved into something complete and great.*</u>

∞ 99 ∞

Mouse can't stop staring at the photo of the lawn.

I want to be kicking that ball SO MUCH. I want to be mucky again, yeah, right filthy with dirt. I want mud caked all over my hands and knees so that when it's washed away I'm new and soft, like I've been magicked alive from a drowning or a burial or something, all clean and sparky and fresh. I want to be running so far and so fast that my side hurts in a stitch and my legs ache and when I wake in the morning the ache is worse like the day after Sports Day and good grief I can't BELIEVE I've just written that.

A little boy pressing his stomach and palms to the wall, then his wet cheek. Trying to press through, press out.

A time to weep, and a time to laugh;
a time to mourn, and a time to dance.

∞ 100 ∞

A piece of toothpaste holds the photograph to the inside of the cupboard wall.

Who'll control the remembering? This hidden place. It's a start. A heartbeat. A heartbeat to battle all the lying and rewriting and forgetting because people have to. They have to move on. It's too hard. They don't want to know. Dad told me. He says it's evolution. It's how the world carries on. And now I get why he asked me to write everything down. He said, 'Tell our story, tell the truth,' because no one else will. And then Mum. 'Mr, if you want to be a writer then you have to make the words leap off the page. Make them like a needle under the skin. Make them get up and shout.' Mum. Yeah. Always so full-on.

He's now ripping every single sheet from his notebook and sticking them onto the cupboard wall with dots of toothpaste, pages and pages, a vast, pale quilt.

THESE THINGS ARE HAPPENING.

The shout of the final sheet.

Too many of us are being disappeared or written out or lost and please, please don't wreck this. Please don't rip this down and throw it out. PLEASE DON'T FORGET US.

All his words in their hidden little harbour and you shut your eyes and turn your back on them, cannot bear it, what you have put him through; for it's as if this cupboard is the only place in the world his precious pages can now, ever, be safe. And he knows it.

> *'Sensible men are all of the same religion.'*
> *'And pray what is that?' . . .*
> *'Sensible men never tell.'*

↶ 101 ↷

Tidge is asleep, the key from Soli locked within the cage of his fingers. Mouse hovers. Tries to lift it away but his brother holds it tighter, still asleep. His sister looks across; he smiles, embarrassed. Asks her what else their father left because the memory box is soaked in their mother and he's sure, *sure*, their dad would have left something more of himself.

'I don't know. There's the doll. What else do you want?'

'Maybe there's something in it. Let's rip it open!'

'It's just a toy. Dad had it as a kid.'

'But why . . . *this*?'

'Because—' She stops. 'It's complicated.' Sighs. 'Dad said he wanted us to have . . . the solace of imagination.' Her eyes screw up with the effort of trying to get it right.

'But what's some manky old doll got to do with it?'

'He wants us to believe that it can help.' She closes her eyes, attempting to slip into her father's words. 'He said that people who have faith have this . . . serenity about them, this strength, that people who believe in nothing just don't. That those kinds of people can be all sour and unhappy and restless and empty, and how horrible is that? He says that people who've reached the pinnacle of their faith, whatever it might be, are at peace. Filled with love and light. And maybe that's a good place to be. Especially now. He says at the heart of any religion is compassion, and it's all we have to get good at. And the doll might remind us. Or something.' She frowns, can't quite remember, looks at her brother; he stares back blank. 'Dad said that at the height of any faith you can feel filled with love and strength and if we got anywhere near that, then, well, it might just help. That's it. I think.'

Mouse rolls his eyes.

'He said people with faith can do amazing things.'

'Amazingly horrible things.'

'Not always, Mr. Sometimes quite the opposite in fact.'

Integrity creates a body so vast a thousand
winged ones will plead,
'May I lay my cheek against you?'

∾ 102 ∾

A knock. Mid-morning. G never knocks.

'Hello? Let me in.'

Your kids look at each other. It is Pin.

'If you don't let me in I'm getting my da-ad.' A taunt in a voice you do not like.

'You can't.' Mouse, fast, signalling to his siblings to be quiet. 'Come back later. This afternoon. At one.' Well done. Because it's B's busy time in the kitchen. Because he never visits them then.

'Why not now?' The voice is stubborn. Argumentative. With the sense of entitlement of an only child. He'd annoy you if he was in their class.

'Because ... we do things at this time. Every day. It's our religion.'

Mouse looks at his siblings.

'Okay,' the voice says mildly.

Your three children high-five each other in astounded silence. Because it worked. Your family hasn't done God for generations, three at least, but he bought it. When Mouse asked you why, once, you were so wary of religion, you told him that you hated all the rules and boring lectures, you thought it was a weakness, a lack of intelligence, you're not into all that dependent thought. 'It's this beautiful, singing lie, my lovely, and eventually all the faiths around us will exist nowhere but the history books.'

Pin doesn't need to know any of that. His religion's burned into his people, by birth they're the warriors of their god. They're fighting your godlessness and greed. They want to stamp it all out with a rage that's soldered into their hearts.

*But now I only hear its melancholy, long,
withdrawing roar.*

❧ 103 ❧

So.

Project Indigo.

You can hardly bear to sew these words into your quilt; you must.

A WMD that specifically targets a certain race. Its formula attacking a peculiarity of their genetic make-up. Preventing them from reproducing. Causing them, mysteriously, to die out. A generation or two is all it will take and then your people will be rid of them, they'll be no more threat. The project so secretive that they'd never know what's stopping their women from falling pregnant, they'll just ... vanish. A natural process. Humane. Clearing them peacefully from your earth. Breeding the stain out. They'll wonder if it's something they're eating, their sexual practices, contaminated water, soil, pesticides, plastics; they'll never know. But it'll stop them multiplying like rabbits and eventually those left will abandon their cursed place; they're superstitious, they'll clear out. And your people will have their country back. So. Peace at last.

The audacity of it, the stun. You can hardly bear to write what you were once. Your hand is trembling.

And you're the only one left with the key to activate it.

'Thwart them all,' Motl joked, long after he'd left the project. 'Lodge your papers in the British Library so they'll all have it, and no one will dare use it. Anyone could convert it for their own use. Imagine that. It'll keep everyone in check.'

'I wouldn't trust a single one of them.' You laughed. 'They'll all grab it. The world will stop.'

'And what gives *you* the right to play God?' His voice, suddenly bereft of any light. Your laughter stopped.

'You don't trust me, do you.' A statement not a question.

'No,' he replied, flat. 'I don't. I think you're dangerous.'

You shawled your arms around your shoulders, swiftly cold, wanting out. How well did you know him? How well did you know anyone? Everyone has a secret life.

And now. The only one left. You hold the key. You, alone, can activate it. You have to get your kids out, you have to get your husband back. You, alone, can activate it. You hold the key. You know what they want. An eye for an eye, a tooth for a tooth, and once, long ago, you craved the glory so much.

The Lord is a man of war.

❧ 104 ❧

Now in their room a new dance begins.

Your children's aim is to ensnare this child from the other side, so he'll never betray them, never give them up. Ensnare him with friendship and trust.

The doctor's boy loves the television. They let him perform a series of operations. He manages, miraculously, a scratch of jittery lines and as he hums away, absorbed, you can sense him revelling in this secret new life. Does he have his own TV? 'Dad doesn't allow it.' Of course. Devout. Walled up. A life rigidly censored, controlled. The path mapped out: a religious school until he was placed under quarantine, an impressionable young mind corralled by holy books. Dependent thought, oh yes.

Yet here he is now, diving deep. As if he's heard about these people but has never seen one up close. Examining the tattoos drawn in pen on arms, your daughter's earrings, the feral hair, clothes, examining the TV like an eighteenth-century surgeon learning from a corpse.

Smart, and you hate that. Always want your kids to be the best. He wears glasses. Talks fast. Uses complicated words, must be often among adults. Can't quite get his head around Soli's vibrant, unknowing ripeness; reddens, often, at her glance.

'This place doesn't let in the sky,' he declares, annoyed, patting the walls of their room like a horse's flank. Perhaps he craves, just like your lot, out; all of them trapped by the adults in their lives. Some people are a force of nature but he's the opposite, he looks like he's spent his entire life in a van with the windows blacked out. All gangly legs and arms, pale, bereft of muscle and tone, watchful, hungry for experience, vividly alone. Just like your childhood once.

You pray as you watch this taut, careful ballet unfolding that his edges have been softened, somewhere, that he's been mellowed by sorrow at some point. Because that will give him compassion. And will give your kids a chance. It's too early to call. You worry about your elder son the most, his enormous, open-hearted trust. Because with that comes loose talk.

What went ye out into the wilderness to see?

༄ 105 ༄

'What's that?' Pin stares in wonder at the memory book.

'Our holy book,' Mouse says fast, coming between it.

Pin nods. Doesn't mention it again. Has no curiosity, doesn't give it another look.

Your holy book, yes. Soaked in love and landscape. And for you that is enough.

I go bound in the spirit.

⌒ 106 ⌒

As Project Indigo came close to fruition Motl chewed his nails down to the bleeding quick. One night, in alarm, you wrapped each fingertip in the cave of your mouth and when you finally drew breath, and sat back, he said, '*Please* can we keep our scientific endeavours at a more humble level, Mrs. You're getting above yourselves here. I *do not like it.*'

'Sssh,' you whispered, kissing a fingertip and pressing it to his lips. 'It's exhilarating. To get this far, as a species, to evolve so much. To unravel the mysteries of creation—'

'I'm not so sure it's called "evolving". And no one can ever explain the biggest question of the lot, Mum: how life was first created on this planet. How this incredibly complex, beautiful world began. I can tell you right now you'll never even get close.'

'Well, I damned well want to try,' you teased. 'I am *loving* this journey, you know that.'

He pulled away. 'Oh, for a simple life.'

'So you've turned all Goddy on me, have you? And which religion is it, my love? The cow, the crescent, the cross?'

'I don't need any of them.' Angry now. 'It's impossible to explain to someone like you. But it's like I'm becoming myself, what I was always meant to be. And I don't need a church for it.' He jabbed his finger in fury. 'People who completely deny spirituality are missing what it is to be fully human – with all its fallibility and mess and stupidity, yes, but all its glory –' his voice breaks 'and beauty.'

'Religious people are either terrorists or paedophiles.'

He sighed. 'There are good people among them. Deeply intelligent, thinking people. They're usually older. They're sometimes near the end of their lives. They have this grace of certainty, and they shine with it. I admire it. I wish I could have it myself. You can extract just the meat from all their books, you know; use them like self-help manuals. Forget the religious nutters – the best people, well, they're discerning. Thinking.' He tapped his temples with both hands. 'They've learned how to glean the sweetest juice from the texts and just toss away the rest. The Bible, the Koran, they're like human life itself: inconsistent. Ridiculous. Infuriating. Good and bad, beautiful and ugly, it's all there. Nothing's black and white, my love, nothing.'

It was your turn to sigh. 'Can we agree to disagree on this one?'

'As long as you respect my choice.'

> *Different creeds are but different paths*
> *to reach the Almighty.*

⊶ 107 ⊷

The doctor's boy turns the scratching from the television into news briefly once; a finger has been grown onto a pig's back. Tidge whoops. 'Hey, dude, can we have *The Simpsons* next?' His arm drapes around the boy's concentrating shoulders and you shiver as you watch. Because he's growing scarily fond of this person in their midst. Who visits every day, who never lets them rest. And who is entirely focused on getting the television to work; who has a discipline that's beyond your rowdy lot.

He has a satellite tracker and an alarm within a complicated watch on his wrist. The four of them huddle under the duvet as he explains it, the dial glowing a luminous green like the bridge of a ship.

'Wow, can I have it?' Tidge teases. 'It'd sure come in handy.' His finger circles it playfully. 'You're coming with us, aren't you?'

'I can?'

A frozen quiet.

Everything suddenly fragile. No one knowing what to say next. Because either this unexploded grenade of a child in their midst hasn't a friend in the world, or he's a very good actor. And none of you can work out which.

Wisdom is the principal thing; therefore get wisdom:
and with all thy getting get understanding.

⤬ 108 ⤬

Are your kids his secret project and he'll eventually haul them off to his father as his triumphant catch? Does he think they're a way to the feral kids outside, to getting them rounded up, the city cleansed of its rats? Does he just want company? Is it as simple as that?

Whatever it is, your children are caught. This persistent boy wants to play, he wants kids to fill up his days and they're forced to go along with it and all you can do is watch. Can't read him. It's rare for a child to be so closed off. You're unnerved by his self-possession. His adult veneer. He likes everything just so; is used to rules; gets upset when your lot bicker among themselves; tells them his ears are hurting and wearily admonishes them to be quiet in a grown-up voice. You bristle with indignation as if a fellow parent has told them off. If he was on a sleepover at your house you'd be worried about what he'd be reporting back; your kids seem so big and naughty and energetic in comparison, slippery and cheeky, uncontained, rough. He'll tell them when they're getting too much, scold them to share, stop the fuss.

He comes from a tight house, you can tell; he's spent his life being reined in, is relentlessly neat, his clothes never bear a mark. He likes discipline. Expects it in others. You can't imagine any other parents liking him except his own; you're so competitive about other kids, really wouldn't need to hear how fabulous he is at everything; which you can see, infuriatingly, would be the case. You wonder about his true self, the veering off-course that exists in everyone, the possibility of an explosion underneath. What he would do if he worked your lot out? He's a tattle-tale, you're sure of that, it's in his voice. The constant worry harangues you night after night.

> *Do not be envious of each other;*
> *and do not outbid each other;*
> *and do not hate each other.*

Bullets. Outside. Not far but not too close. A conversation of rat tat tats.

'Kalashnikov,' Pin, knowingly.

'Three blocks away,' Tidge, 'tank attack.'

'Raid,' Mouse, 'resistance.' The noise changes to short pops.

'Pistols!' The boys all laugh. 'Snap!' And the three of them fire pretend machine guns out the window.

Soli's alone in a handstand against the wall. 'So who exactly are we fighting, guys,' she languidly enquires, 'when we're out of this place?'

'Your lot.' Tidge giggles at Pin. 'You got us into this mess.'

'Excuse me, *your* lot are the baddies.'

'I beg your pardon?' Soli arcs gracefully up.

'We're the ones trying to fix this country.'

Your kids stop, stunned. 'Have you *been* out there?' Your daughter angrily asks. 'Have you *seen* what's happening?'

Pin covers his ears and chants la la la and Tidge strides into the thick of it with arms outstretched and says, 'Stop, guys, *stop*,' because he hates conflict. 'Let's make a gang,' he announces, 'top secret,' all the while looking at his sister, pleading with her. 'Let's say ... the Getters, huh?' because the friendship has to be maintained, because it's the only way out.

'Okay,' Soli says finally.

'Rule number one,' Tidge announces gleefully, 'no one gets left behind! We can never abandon a Getter comrade.'

'Or betray them,' Mouse adds drily.

Pin jokes that it's how his father got ahead and Soli says this isn't the grown-up world, they're far too screwed up for us and Pin rolls his eyes and smiles and you wonder about that adult sneer, you wonder what he's gleaning in this place. Tidge says he's got a secret handshake and he takes the left hand of Pin and places it palm down on his right. Squeezes. 'Your turn,' he says, and the boy takes his hand and does the same and Mouse takes Soli's and smiles secrets at her and apologies and regret. She smiles, warm, back. 'No one gets left behind,' she whispers fierce, trying to bind all four of them, blood-tight, to strengthen around this frail quartet a net of friendship that will hold firm.

'Hey, we've got to do that blood thing, too!' Pin says. 'You know, where you prick your fingers. Blood brothers. Seizing the day and all that. Come on.'

Your children groan. But do it because they must.

Ye fathers, provoke not your children to wrath.

✌ 110 ✌

His smile turns him into someone else. They coax it from him whenever they can. To become human to the enemy not objects of hate, you've drilled into them the importance of that. He's not laughed once while he's with them. 'Am I that unfunny?' Mouse finally enquires.

'Yep.'

Your boy drops to the ground, flings his arms wide, waits to be shot.

'No! I mustn't laugh. It's my asthma. It restricts my breathing. The doctor says I shouldn't risk it. I haven't laughed for ages. I'm aiming for the *Guinness Book of Records*. You watch.'

'You're kidding,' Tidge says, his eyes dancing up.

'I'm serious,' Pin protests. 'I've got an inhaler and everything.'

'It's all in your head,' Soli declares.

And so the covert mission begins. To get him laughing, to get that shirt hanging out and the hair mussed up. Alphabet burping, gurning, flicking coins from elbows, break-dancing on their heads, all B's tricks. Pin stares as if they're the most peculiar children he's ever met. They persist. Mouse flips his eyelids inside out until they hurt like a contact lens dried up. Pin's mouth curls, a bloom spreads across his cheeks. 'Ah ha!' Soli points in triumph and Mouse flips his eyelids back. They'll have him yet.

A threefold cord is not quickly broken.

∽ 111 ∾

'You're really lucky, you know.'

'Um, why Pin?'

'Because no one's ever telling you what to do. You can stay awake until midnight if you want. And you never have to do your homework, or eat broccoli, or wear a button shirt.'

'Yeah, but it's horrible not having a home to go to,' Mouse shoots back. 'We have this football, on our lawn, that's waiting for us . . .' He pauses, your heart races.

'Don't give up,' Pin says in rescue.

A shining quiet.

'You're really lucky your dad says goodnight to you every night,' Tidge says finally, soft. 'Ours used to do that. Blow out the light, he'd say, like it was a candle, and it'd turn off exactly when we puffed.'

'You can have mine too if you want! He'll adopt you.'

Your children smile. Because it's a start. A ridiculous one but a start nonetheless. And this stranger in their midst seems to have a quality their father loves so much – *empathy* – and he'd be punching the air at that. He despises callousness because he says it's a failure of the imagination, a failure to put yourself in someone else's place.

'No one gets left behind,' Soli suddenly whispers, and each

203

child puts a palm on a hand and squeezes tight.
  In the shining quiet.

  Take away love and our earth is a tomb.

∞ 112 ∞

But their nights. Stained by scrawny sleep. Addled by B's vanishing. What could have happened? Was this abandonment planned? Is he hurt, discovered, gone? His apples are pitted like old people's faces with no teeth, even the flies have left in disgust. The fruit growing its fur is the last of him left.

'We'll have to throw it out, guys,' Soli instructs.

'No,' Mouse pleads, 'please.'

'Why?'

'Because B is a thread to Mum and Dad. The *only* thread we've got left. Without him they're gone . . . and we're all alone.'

'It's going to be all right. Dad promised he'd come, he *promised*.'

But her voice betrays she no longer believes it.

Be islands of refuge unto yourselves.

❧ 113 ❧

'Maybe we're meant to be sorting this out for ourselves.' Tidge is sitting under the window holding the doll. 'Maybe Pin can help. What do you think, guys?'

'Uh-uh.' Soli rushes in. 'Do not even go there.'

'Why?'

She squats in front of him. 'Because we can't have your little mate knowing about B for a start. No matter how friendly he might seem he's his father's son. Always. Never forget that. He's not meant to know people like us, let alone be our friend. We can't have his dad *ever* knowing about this room. It would be disastrous.'

Tidge gazes out of the window. 'There are street kids out there. I've seen them.'

'I have too.' She stands behind him. 'But it doesn't mean they've got a better life.'

'It'd be more friends. And a step closer to home. And maybe Pin could come too, maybe he wants a different life, just like us. You don't know him. You're not *listening* to me, you're not listening.'

Soli makes a little kissing noise of disapproval and runs her fingers up the huff of her brother's back.

Experts are agreed that the man who labels things 'bad'
is thereby making it impossible for himself
to see them as they really are.

❦ 114 ❦

He never behaves like he's meant to. His hackles don't rise when he sees them. He never humiliates them; it's as if they're just kids, nothing else; he's not seeing anything different; not seeing a colour or a religion or a race. You can't get your head around it. It can't be this simple. 'I feel the opposite of lonely here,' he says with a smile one day, flopping on the bed, 'whatever that is. Filled up.'

He brings gifts. They start anticipating his arrival. For Tidge, any stick-like object that has the potential to be a sword. For Soli, nail polish and glitter pens. For Mouse, one time, a strange white sphere with green stains.

'Um, thanks. What is it?'

'A pukka. For polo. It's the only ball I could find. Until you can get your other one back.'

'Huh?'

'The one on the lawn. That's waiting for you.'

Heart, swell.

'Gee. Thanks. But I can't catch, you know.'

'Mate, you are *all* talk.'

'I can't catch, Pin.'

The boy lobs the ball and Mouse reaches up and snatches it crisp; 'eeeeh,' he squeals and Pin stands there smiling, all his paleness gone and colour in his cheeks, and your daughter's staring with her hands on hips, nodding, appreciating. 'There you go.' He laughs. 'What did I tell you, dude?' grinning at little

Mouse who's responding with, 'Thanks, mate, thanks,' over and over, he can't stop. Because he's feeling quite someone else, suddenly, someone better and bigger and straighter than himself. Because he caught a ball, the cool way, overhand, and he's never done that. His smile is one huge watermelon split. Because no boy except his brother has ever looked at him like this. Like he's whole. And in that golden moment your awkward, self-conscious, clotted little Mouse has his entire world filled up and you love this stranger for that, you will never forget it. Something has changed in this room, loosened; you'd battened down the hatches for so long but now, softly, something is breaking out.

How great a matter a little fire kindleth.

⧸ 115 ⧹

What is this brightening within you, what? Like a varnisher's hand passed over a painting, you feel plumed with light. Combusted into peace and stillness and rest. It is so calming and strong through you.

A chink, just a chink, into Motl's momentous journey. Something like the beginning of an understanding, yes.

More things are shewed unto thee than men understand.

❧ 116 ❧

'So what's your dad *really* like?' Tidge, nonchalantly, as all four of them are lying on their backs on the bed, counting spots on the ceiling, and everyone's getting a different amount.

'What do you mean?' A new voice.

Careful, Tidgy, tread light. Not now.

'Well, you know' – he skates merrily on – 'sometimes you can love a person, but not really . . . like them. Know what I mean?'

'Pardon?' Pin sits up. A stoplight in his voice.

Mouse covers his face with his hands, grimacing, needing his klutzy pickaxe of a brother to stop this right now, fast.

'My father's done a lot for this country.'

'But my mum says if no one speaks out . . . then lies become truth. And the truth can get lost.'

Oh, boy, boy, boy.

'So what exactly does he *do*, your dad, can he help us?'

'Do? He works incredibly hard to make this country a better place. And it's not easy with people like you. We need men like him. He says he'll die working because of me.'

'To keep you in computer games,' Mouse throws in, trying to loosen everything up.

'Thank you, yes.'

'But do you have any idea what's really going on? Really truly?' Tidge persists.

'Would you like to see? His baby is the Persuasion Unit. Have you heard of it? I can arrange for you to be shown if you'd like.' The voice with the grown-up already in it.

'No thank you,' Tidge murmurs.

Soli's hand is at her mouth like she's going to be sick.

Mouse rolls away from them all and curls tight on the edge of the bed. Because he's heard of this Persuasion Unit, late at night, when Motl and you have been talking about your country and then you've stopped and gone very quiet and the weight of that place has sat between you and your little boy has felt very cold, and small, and stunned, in his hiding hole under the stairs, winded by the listening and knowing he shouldn't be eavesdropping on your talk let alone writing it down. He should be tucked in his bed in the warm snuggly quiet, not knowing any of this. What grown-ups do. When they've lost their light hearts.

Pin gets up. Walks out. All the cosiness in their room vanished like a candle blown out. Your heart pebbles with it.

Do battle against them until there be no more seduction from the truth.

∞ 117 ∞

'You consider us as nothing more than mosquitoes. Not human beings. It's as though we don't exist as people to you.' What one of them said to you once.

'And what do you consider us?' you managed to stumble, wrong-footed, in response. Thinking of the rhetoric that inflamed your country then inflamed your work: 'Do unto them now as they shall surely do to you tomorrow.' We are all animal underneath. And some of us, abhorrently, are given the licence to release it. *Why* were you so seduced? You were always so puzzled, in your twenties, by Yeats' words, 'the worst are full of passionate intensity.' How come the 'worst'? Surely he'd made a mistake, surely it's what you must be?

Now you get it.

And you have learned that a life unchanged is a life unlived. You hate what you were once. If only you could wash it all away like mud under a shower, and start again clean, afresh. You can finally admit that there have been mistakes in your past, catastrophic errors of judgement, and they have affected not only you but others, so many others around you, and you never thought enough about that. Blinded by zeal, rampantly ambitious, swept away by inflaming sentiment; narrow, judge-mental, righteous, tough. You know now that ageing is about embracing fallibility, in yourself and in others. You think of those elderly people you have sometimes come across – men, mostly, from various walks of life – who glow with an accumulation of good living. Full of juice. Free of judgement. Joyous, chuckly, chuffed; surrendering to the chaos of it all, and the wonder. A completeness to them, a richness, from all they have learned in life.

Catastrophic errors of judgement. And now you, and others, must pay for them.

So. This. The boy from the other side gone. In fury. Your children tremulously quiet. Everything careful, fragile, stopped. Talk blown out of them with what on earth's coming next. It's been so long since you've heard Mouse's whistling, Soli's singing, Tidge's laugh and you ache for them, *ache* for them, and breathing is now tight in your chest, as if a giant hand is twisting your heart and squeezing it, as if you are rising on a great dark wing and it is blackening out the sun and there is no good air left. You wait. All of you. Will he come back? Will he tell his father? What is next? This room is nobody's friend, not even a clock's tick breaks its mausoleum quiet; the dark is curtain-thick, no light any more, from any source.

The very purpose of religion is to control yourself,
not to criticise others.
Rather, we must criticise ourselves.
How much am I doing about my anger?
About my attachment, about my hatred,
about my pride, my jealousy?

❧ 118 ❧

The door. A key. B. It must be. Relief and fury that he's left them so long.

It is Motl. Bursting through the door like he's been blasted in by some explosive force.

You stagger. Your lovely man, before you.

Back, given back.

How vividly he's been distilled in his vanishing, in such a short time, to a few precious snippets now riveted into your heart: a photo of him, nonchalant on a country railway track; his smell, hair oil; the burst of his laugh; the luxurious sweep of his handwriting; the way he says 'yeah' at you, sceptically; a silly winter hat. The feel of his fingers slipping into your pants after you've been loosened by a night out with girlfriends and your insides peel away at his touch – you will always have the sensation of it – your groin softly contracting, then bucking, opening out into his palm, offering wetness. God, that he can still have that effect on you, after fifteen years of marriage, this man, this gift. In the thick of an argument you've flung all manner of stupid taunts, 'I hate you' and 'I want a divorce' and 'Get me out' but he knows you never mean it although his eyes are always hurt. So much gratitude unexpressed. That you've been so blessed. He is a good man, he has given you so much, and you've never properly told him that.

And now, and now.

Returned. To the children. Alive. In one piece. You shut your eyes, all you want to do is hold him, just hold him, breathing him in, then later spoon, silently, in your nightly ritual that has concluded every night of your married life; with your belly pressed into his back and then he whispers 'seatbelt' and you obediently turn and offer him the expanse of your own back and his arm slots over yours and he nestles in and exhales a long contented breath as if he has waited all day for this moment of rest. Days. Weeks. And here he is. The marvel of it. The love that is an accumulation of years of conversations and fights and making-ups, a first tremulous fuck and matching, extremely cheap wedding rings and Friday night takeaways and weekends in unaffordable hotels but what the heck and concerts where the highly anticipated performer is drunk and grainy ultrasound pictures and labour wards and car trips with 'Are we there yet?' endlessly from the back and watching in awe the three children created together, peacefully asleep, and laughter, so much laughter, yes that. The key, you think: that he still makes you laugh. Both of you came to the same conclusion not too far back, that the secret to life is to wring as much happiness as you can out of your time on this earth. And often that happiness is found in the simplest moments.

The four of them. It's all you need, want.

I thirst.

215

❦ 119 ❧

Motl smiles as he opens out his arms to his squealy children.

'*Daaaaaaaad!*'

Back. Just as he promised. Your heart hurts with love. The sight of that little huddle; it, too, is riveted within you; it will never be lost.

Pre-Salt Cottage, when he'd stay out late with mates, you used to panic as the hours ticked on past midnight; perhaps he's dead, been mugged, you'd think. Then you'd weigh up your world without him and a part of you would breathe out in relief: 'Ah, free again.' To be the woman you once were; to run your life as you want. Decorate the house your way entirely, eat like a single woman, give the kids cereal for dinner, discipline them with no one to counter it. But the sweetness of that moment when you heard the key in the lock! Back, safe. The person who understands you more than any other in your life. As eccentric as you despite being complete opposites, and if you didn't have him you wouldn't have anyone else.

And now, and now. You hover a touching, it hurts. He's changed, you frown. A beard and he's never had that. It alters him completely. 'I know' – he throws up his hands in disgust – 'I'm a prisoner in my face.' He tries to scrabble it off as the children climb all over him. But he looks wrong. It isn't just the whiskers – he looks like a child someone has dressed too fast. The coat is buttoned into holes that don't match, the socks are different colours, the hair is unbrushed. He's lost weight.

He's filthy. But most wrong of all is the light: it's gone from his eyes. Like he's been snuffed. He's never been this.

'Are you okay . . . Dad?' Mouse asks.

Motl grins. 'It's been a mighty long journey to get to you lot. But hey, I'm here. And soon we'll be out of this place. I just need a quick kip, and then we're off!'

Mouse hugs him tight. Hugs into him all his relief and joy and hope. Feel this, says his fierce press. Our whole future is in it. You drop to your knees; prayer is gratitude, oh yes. He's a wonderful father, always has been. They'll be all right, they'll be all right.

Twenty of you who stand firm shall vanquish two hundred.

⤜ 120 ⤛

How soon they settle into the old ways, how quickly normality is back. Explanations and jokes and an apology to pass on, from B, for not being here; he's been madly busy getting another family safe and things haven't gone according to plan, there were complications. And then Motl holds up his hands to all the questions; yes, yes, Mum is alive, she's okay, don't worry, B's assured him you're all right, you're just sorting out a few things and as he speaks he looks straight at you, suddenly, straight into you, as if he knows, and you shake your head and in a blink he's back at them; you must have imagined it; hang on, he's laughing, aren't there three starving mouths to be fed in this place? B has helped, snuck him in, has even let him deliver this trolley; it's highly dangerous but what the heck, Motl had to get to them, had to. 'I promised, didn't I?' and then he sweeps his hand across three silver domes and it is everything the children could want.

He salutes, clicks his heels. 'For my big, brave soldiers – only the best.'

The children dive in. In the thick of it Soli puts down her milkshake and takes her father's hand and encases it in both of hers like it is a fragile, injured animal; like she is the grown-up in all this. She leads him to the bed and pats a space beside her. His face looks old, now, for the first time in his life; suddenly it is allowed to be that. All his impishness is blown out. His eyes are reddened like they've been scrubbed with steel wool, his hands tremble as if still in shock. How can such a large-spirited man be so reduced? What happened out there? He pulls away as if he can see inside her thinking and doesn't like it. Flops onto his back. His face irons out.

'Eat, my lovelies,' he says wearily now, bereft of any spark, 'come on, you need to build up your strength. We've got a big journey ahead of us.'

Soli places her cardigan gently over his shoulders and he draws it around him like it's the finest mink then closes his eyes with a contented sigh, as if it's the first time he's closed them in a week.

Who, being loved, is poor?

∽ 121 ∽

B has assured him you're all right, you're just sorting out a few things.

And what does that man know of you being here? You always suspected he knew of Project Indigo; you've never been entirely sure who he works for, where his allegiances lie. You asked Motl once what his religion was. 'He was one of them, years ago,' he replied. 'Now I don't know. I'm not sure he works for anyone any more. He's a humanitarian, I guess. He works for humanity's sake.'

He's never completely trusted you just as you've never trusted him. When you announced you were giving up your job B retorted he didn't believe it would last, your resolve wasn't strong enough, you'd eventually be lured back. 'You're so *driven*,' and he made it sound like a dirty word. 'You want it too much,' the dismissive taunt.

Anger now, anger at all of this. You know what they want. You have been found and they want you to complete the project. All as cruel as each other, all animal underneath.

> *Tranquil sage is he who, whether young,*
> *middle-aged or old,*
> *remains firm in self-restraint,*
> *unprovokable, provoking none.*

❧ 122 ❧

Soli is furiously tapping her watch. It is almost two. And who knows if Pin will be back but the risk is there: they need their father out.

Mouse nods at his sister, understands, licks his lips. 'We have to move fast, Dad. It's so dangerous you being here . . .'

'Not yet.' Motl is yawning, slipping into slumber almost caught. 'I can't move another step, Mousie, I just need . . . rest.' His whole body is uncurling, shutting down. He releases an enormous groan as if all the dammed-up tension of the past weeks is finally, finally seeping out, as if this room is the only place in the world he can rest.

'You can't stay here!' Soli cries. 'We have to move you. Move all of us. *Now*.'

'Yes, yes, in a minute.' Motl yawns, your old procrastinator back, flattening both hands under one cheek. 'Things are changing, guys,' he's murmuring, 'help is coming from unexpected places, I have a good feeling . . .' His eyes shut slowly, he is lost.

Two minutes to two. What to do? A petal is on his boot, a white one, just like the ones at Salt Cottage. They haven't seen anything like it for so long and soon it will be crushed to translucency and Mouse peels it off and Motl smiles at his son's hovering, and falls vastly asleep. Soli shakes him. He doesn't

221

respond, all flop. His body is devouring recovery, rest is gripping him tight, refusing to give him up, sleep has him too much.

*Why ever trouble your heart with flight
when you have just arrived.*

❧ 123 ❧

A knock. Two on the dot. The children look at each other. Soli revs her hand in circles, trying to think of something but can't, can't; the doorknob turns. Opens. *Opens.*

Pin is standing there, before them, with a sheepish grin and an apologetic box of chocolates and some chewing gum and it all comes crashing to the ground. As he sees the new man. They don't even have time to throw a blanket over Motl smiling away in his enormous relief of sleep.

But Pin's face. Like a cloud racing over sunlight. He steps back. 'Who is this?' Like a thick glass wall in a bank has suddenly shot up.

'Wait,' Tidge cries, but Pin holds up his hands, all changed.

'You're not who I think you are, are you?' He glances to the door, wants away, wants help.

Your mouth is dry, you feel sick. Everything is unravelling. Mouse lunges. Grabs the key, locks the door, trapping Pin inside. Oh, little man, brave man, finally waking up.

'What are you *doing*?' Pin yells.

Mouse holds out his hand as to a dog about to bite, trying to calm him, to get him to sit. 'You're our friend,' he says carefully.

But Pin doesn't want to know, he's gripping his watch with the alarm that pinpoints his location; he hasn't pressed it yet.

'No one gets left behind,' your daughter pleads, 'we're the Getters, we're in this together.'

'You're our *friend*,' Tidge yells with disbelieving shock, at being betrayed, at being so wrong, standing tall on the bed. 'You're my mate.'

Pin presses the alarm. 'My father can sort this out.'

Tidge's knees sink to the mattress. Mouse slumps against the wall. You shut your eyes on everything ahead, that Motl and you have feared so much. G's plan was such a risk but you both had to accept it, there was no one else, *no safe house left.* And now this. Your lovely sparky vivid-hearted babies sizzly with life will be separated and your boys, all three of them, will be taken to that place where men go on the edge of the city and your daughter will never find out what happened and for the rest of her life she'll be wondering, crazed by uncertainty, wondering about trembling pits and being broken and what on earth happened next.

> *In the darkness . . . the sound of a man*
> *Breathing, testing his faith*
> *On emptiness, nailing his questions*
> *One by one to an untenanted cross.*

∞ 124 ∞

'Mummy?' Tidge asks.

It is his voice from late at night when he has just had a nightmare and you come, you always come, and you encase him in your warmth. 'Mummy?' he asks again and a hopelessness washes over you and dumps you like a wave in the surf.

Your daughter balls her hand and holds it trembling to her face. You know why. She wants to hit Pin just like she hit her father once, after the soldiers came, wants to wallop into him all her howling at the unfairness of this world.

Mouse throws a bowl of ice cream onto his father's face. He splutters awake. 'Soldiers are coming,' Mouse shouts, 'get out.'

Motl looks around, shakes sleep from his head. Sees Pin. 'What the—'

'We'll look after him,' Soli says, 'just *go*.' She pushes her father to the door. 'Come *on*,' she yells into his resisting weight.

'I can't.' He squats close to her face. Brushes her cheek, slowly, with his thumb; all the world's tenderness in it. 'I promised your mother I'd never abandon you.'

She pummels him. 'Just *go*,' her voice choked.

Tidge grabs the doll, throws it onto the trolley, pushes it against the door and locks the wheels.

'It's no use,' Pin smirks, 'it's not keeping anyone out.' His heart now closed whereas once – at flopping on their bed, at throwing a ball – it was open, full, soft.

'*You*' – your daughter turns on him – 'what happened to the Getters? To no one gets left behind?'

He bats her away.

'We weren't harming anyone. We just want our parents back. You have no idea what it's like.' She points at Motl. 'He's never hurt anyone, he's good, he has a *heart*.' She thumps her palm at her chest.

'I do too,' Pin yells back. 'I *trusted* you.'

'Well, if you do have a heart,' Motl says evenly, 'then show it.'

And quick as a flash he's behind him and whipping off his watch like a Fagin who's perfected the technique through years of silky theft. It's thrown onto the bed. Motl then places his hand firmly around the boy's mouth and kicks the trolley away. Tidge grabs the doll. Mouse the memory box. Unlocks the door.

They're off. They have a chance.

Guide our feet unto ways of peace.

∽ 125 ∽

The small wedge of dark under the stairs. Footsteps above, pounding. One set stops on the step above them, patrolling an escape route, the rest run to the deserted room. 'What the . . .' A frustrated shout. The door is kicked. Pin's eyes shine a new hardness in the dark. Sweat trickles. Balances on the end of Tidge's nose. He needs to sneeze. Reaches across to Mouse's hand and wipes the sweat with it and does not let go as feet, so many, race along corridors and kick in doors. The last pair step out of the abandoned room. Slowly, trying to work them out. The footsteps stop. Silence. Too long. Mouse shuts his eyes and mouths *go away go away* and the footsteps move off with thinking in their steps.

Unfurl the relief! Like a banner pluming into bright air! They are safe, they are safe.

The footsteps brisk up the steps and the noises fade and your little group uncurls except for the hand still firmly around Pin's mouth. Then Tidge steps back. Hard onto Mouse's foot. Who swallows a yelp. But drops the memory box.

It crashes to the ground.

They can only watch.

> *But the children of the kingdom*
> *shall be cast out into outer darkness.*

❦ 126 ❦

So. This. The footsteps stopping, turning back. Your little group, your precious little group, cornered. Motl smiling his cheeky smile as the security forces, so many, gather around them. 'You took your time.' He checks his watch. 'Six minutes. What do you reckon, team?' He looks at the children, grabs Pin warmly by the shoulders. 'See, it works.'

The soldiers bristle. 'Leave the boy alone,' the commander says. 'Move away.' A face that sinks your heart. Because it is like a fully human man is not there at all, the person inside has been lost.

'It's a game.' Motl chuckles. 'We wanted to see if that fancy watch of his really works.'

The captain's eyes peer hard at Pin then hard into the rest of them.

'They're all mates,' Motl goes on. 'The boy wanted some friends. He ordered them in. Takeout, if you like. 'I'm with them. We're just mucking about.' A bubble of pink emerges from Motl's mouth and is smartly popped and his eyes do not waver nor the calm in his voice.

'Back, behind us,' the leader barks and obediently Pin scuttles to the rear without looking at any of his friends and in his silence all your original suspicions are firmed: that he was going to do this all along, that he's his father's son, that the city will be rid of its rats, that they will win this.

And now also the axe is laid unto the root of the trees.

228

∞ 127 ∞

Your body. Caving in upon itself. Because now they are lined up against the tiles. Spaced too far apart. Not allowed to touch. Your good man and each of your children so small and thin, as pale as bone, too young for this. Their shoulder blades where their angel's wings once were are pressed hard into the cold and Mouse needs his father's hand now, so much, he's drumming his fingers in a nervous shake, reaching across, and now, and now, a gun is at each of them, each, all aimed straight into their huge racing hearts.

So.
    It has come to this.
    What men do.
    To children.
    And good men.

> *Mine hour is not yet come.*
> *Mine hour is not yet come.*
> *Mine hour is not yet come.*
> *Mine hour is not yet come.*

❧ 128 ❧

'What's *really* going on here?'

There is a smallness about the captain, a terrible banality; he could have been an accountant in a former life. But he has a gun. And that, of course, changes everything. Your husband is elegantly calm, even daring another bubble-gum pop.

'I haven't a clue what their real names are. They've forgotten them. They could be anyone, from any side, any religion, they're shell-shocked. Your boy' – he indicates Pin – 'saw them and snuck them in. They play together. I've come to get my lot out, I don't want them here, I want them back on the streets.' He sighs. 'I like kids. I help them. They help me . . . forget.'

'Who *are* you all?'

'I found them on the street. They've been living rough. They have names, nicknames, that's all I know.' And he gives the secret family names that only the two of you use for them, to comfort, to cherish, to envelop, that are sewn deep into the fabric of this quilt and into your heart. And the captain raises his gun and your Motl grins his easy roguish smile and says, 'Let them go; as for me, well, you can do what you want,' and at that, the butt of the pistol is rammed hard at his face.

His beautiful face.

A rag doll, sliding into a stop, eyes rolling, so much blood so much blood so much blood. All the children rush to him but, '*Don't!*' the captain barks, whipping the pistol back. 'Get him out,' he says to a sidekick and your Motl's weight is lifted by two soldiers like a sack of rubbish now and one soldier doesn't have a proper grip and your man, your darling man, is slipping messily to the floor and is hauled up again and pulled along the corridor, with great effort, as if his entire body has sucked into it some enormous, unearthly weight, his final taunt, and his feet in their old green sneakers are dragged through the sticky wet, so much, smearing it in great red streaky tyre tracks and his rag doll slump follows the black pipes of the ceiling that disappear into the building's dark humming heart and he raises his head, once, and that gives you hope, there is life, life, life, and then his sneakers bounce like a puppet's and turn a corner and snag and are yanked free and are gone. Gone.

Everything, suddenly, is very still. As if something has been blown out. A great goodness, a huge force.

'Daddy!' Tidge howls, 'Daddy, Daddy, Daddy.'

The angels know you well.

❧ 129 ❧

So. Now this. Your three children. It is as if they have been suspended on an ocean liner docked by a wharf and have been holding their streamers tight and the crepe paper has been stretching and stretching but suddenly it has broken, fluttered off, and the ship is now pulling away and they are departing on a journey across a dark ocean to goodness knows what. Alone. The captain comes up close. Mouse's lip shakes. The man tries wrenching the doll from Tidge but Mouse yells no and Soli lunges and they cling like animals possessed. 'Interesting.' The man steps back. He turns to the memory box. Mouse holds it tighter. The captain signals a soldier, the man grabs it, Mouse will not let go, the soldier wrenches. Mouse bites him.

A blow. Across his head. He's all right, okay, he's trying to right himself, the boxer determined not to drop. A trickle slides like an egg down his head; he holds up his hand: it is blood. But the box he will not let go of and a man is prising his fingers from it and his knuckles are bone-white. A karate chop. The memory box is dropped. He presses his hands hard into his head as if he's trying to stop bits coming out and his legs give way and from the ground he watches as fevery fingers tear through your box; hands fling earrings and rip apart the manicure set, flick your last spotty teacup at the wall and smash it to bits; all going, everything lost, every last bit of your Salt Cottage life. But you have prepared for this. Nothing can give them away; it is all anonymous.

232

The captain wheels around, grabs your girl and pulls her roughly to him. Hello hello, he says, *this* is what I was looking for, and holds out her chin in a savage V. Breathes hard into her and yanks back her hair exposing her lovely, pale, vulnerable neck and he stretches out an earlobe and rubs up close.

But her ears.

Of course.

They've won.

Suddenly cold, and tired, and extinguished. Because they now have their excuse to disappear the children too.

Soli has pierced ears.

She did it with her best friend when she was nine, with a needle and a potato and an icy pole to numb the pain, because she wanted to be a pop star when she was grown up. But the religion of these people teaches them that to change God's gift of a body in any way, to prick it or pierce it or colour it, is a sin. Ear piercings always give you away; and tattoos, and face lifts, and dyed hair. It was why the screw-on earrings were the only ones you'd put into the memory box.

The contempt in the man's face, and something else — as he rubs up close to your beautiful, vivid, enchanting girl – the dirt in it.

*Her ways are ways of pleasantness,
and all her paths are peace.*

233

❧ 130 ❧

Raw, open to the bitter wind, skinned. You drop to your knees.
You shut your eyes.

Who is on my side? Who?

❧ 131 ❧

'The Collection Room. Now.' The Collection Room. The Collection Room. And what, pray, do they collect in it? Tears, confessions, blood? The shift of his men tells you it is not a place for children. The yell of Mouse's thinking. He can't take it any more, it's too hard; he shivers, it consumes his tiny frame; his lips are shaky like he's just come out of a freezing pool and there's no towel and the wind's hurting and he's going to cry because it's the only thing left and he looks across to Soli and sobs, now, it's all coming out.

'Wait.'

A tiny voice. Somewhere up the back.

'You can't.'

Pin. Stepping strongly through his men. 'Not the Collection Room. Not that.'

'Excuse me?' The captain smiles, incredulous.

Pin takes a deep breath. 'That man. He was right.'

Everything, suddenly, is very quiet. As if the world has caught its breath.

'They're just kids. From the street. I wanted to play. I saw them. I brought them in. This is all my fault.' He wipes his palms on his trousers. 'I want it stopped now. Please.'

'What would your father make of this?'

Pin lifts his chin. 'My father. Yes. He'll deal with it.'

A tic in the leader's eyelid begins to jump. 'Yes, he will, absolutely.' He nods.

So, the doctor. You knew it would one day come to this. From the moment that boy stepped into their lives. There is only one conclusion; you can hardly bear to think of it. For you know that man better than his son. For you are an adult.

And after the fire a still small voice.

∽ 132 ∞

Now, a room long gone from your country's life.

The walls jade. The floor jade. The ceiling jade.

Your children bunch back, spooked, then like horses at water hesitantly step in. Disbelieving, wondrous, for it is like walking underwater in a shimmering light. Your elder boy laughs out loud despite himself, at the outrageous beauty before him; he forgets himself and runs to a wall and smooths a hand along it in amazement: such secret gorgeousness, in a city so smashed. How? Enormous jade panels have been peeled away from some palace long lost and meticulously pieced back together, from some time long ago when beauty was seen as the pinnacle of human life and the supreme manifestation of godliness and your poor broken country was so good at that once. Beauty, to soar people's hearts. But now. A land where gardeners and flower beds have been abolished as frivolous, along with galleries of antiquities and the film industry and multiple channels on television sets.

But this. A room flooded with sunlight. Three tall windows standing like sentinels across from your children. Outside, a beckoning blue. The three of them step further into this room, open-mouthed, closer, closer to out.

Babylon is fallen, fallen, that great city.

❦ 133 ❦

A man watching them. Pin's father. Of course. They do not see him at first. You remember what B said once: that clinicide involved three types of murder – serial killing, treatment killing and political killing – and this man is an exponent of the latter. 'Doctors murder more than any other group,' B warned, 'never forget that. Let's hope your paths never cross.' And this man would be particularly interested in you, a scientist, your line of work.

And now. In a corner near the door, not moving, watching your children's eyes. What they are resting on, what they are noticing about a way out. How quick they are, how adult, how worn or alert. He is startlingly handsome, but in a way that makes a woman wary; you had a colleague like that once, a man who'd never had to strive at life, who'd been adored by his mother and every woman after her so he'd never had to try, didn't understand failure, had never had to reveal a vulnerable heart. Men who've not grown into fully fledged humans. He'd be a lonely fuck. He could never be taught. Coldness is what you remember about your former colleague the most. And vanity. This, too, is a man who cares about his appearance. His hair has been ploughed severely with a comb. His cuffs are glary white.

Tidge meets his gaze. Your boy does not flinch. Because he knows something this man knows also: that his son is theirs, for the moment, and it may not last but they have him now, just. Careful, brave boy, tread light. Because this man's eyes are the eyes of a winner. Well, well, says Tidge's stare, we'll see about that. But how on earth can a child compete?

Pin comes in last. In a glance you have caught the raw man, the one under all that suit, the furnace inside that his eyes do not match. He loves this boy. You know that love, the way a child can fill a heart.

Pin is pre-teenage-scowly, dismissive. 'It was nothing, Dad, a silly mistake.'

Through love a king is made a slave.

And now the father turns to what stole the son. He scrutinises the general stain of your children and they shrink back at what is vivid in his face. Hate. They are rats, mosquitoes, swattable, nothing; beneath human. And hatred at the leaking of your ways into his son, at the daring to lure him across. But there is something else too and you lean: it is the look of someone threatened. You saw exactly that face, years ago, as a child yourself, in the father of a girl in your class who was pushed to be the best and he never let up with his pushing and one day you beat her in a test and then did it again, and her father marked you out from that time, marked you out with his hatred, wanted you vanished from the grand plan of his daughter's life. Grownups aren't meant to look at children like that but they do. And in Pin's embarrassed scowl now is the beginning of something this man dreads. A boy newly questioning the ideology that has spined his entire existence; journeying into the terrain of skittery, independent thought. And their holy book above all holy books thunders against the tempters who whisper into hearts. *Question everything*, oh yes.

> *Though they learn it all by heart, but fail to study*
> *its import – learning by rote –*
> *they do so to their lasting hurt and ill.*

❧ 135 ❧

The man brisks over to a desk. He takes a small pistol from his drawer, a Tokarev with a mother-of-pearl handle, obviously cherished; he aims it aims it at Tidge's head. This man is an affront to his god. Undo this dark, undo it.

Mouse begins to speak.

'Silence,' the man erupts.

'Dad,' his son interjects.

'Watch this, son.'

'They're just kids.'

'No, you don't understand, it's not what they do now it's what they'll grow into. Do unto them now as they shall do to us tomorrow, remember,' and he is quoting the words of your own people, what you have said many times yourself. 'Have you forgotten what they have done to us?'

'They're my friends, Dad. They're just kids. *Listen* to me.'

But he does not respond, does not hear; one less of them one less and you were that once, you recognise it; wanted them all removed, gone from your life, he as grubby as you, both of you, both.

> *Offensive acts come back upon the evil doer*
> *like dust that is thrown against the wind.*

❧ 136 ❧

'Sir, permission to speak, *sir.*'

Everyone turns. It is the captain who dealt with Motl.

'Granted.'

The doctor annoyed, not wanting interruption, enjoying this.

'There's a doll.'

'What?'

'A suspicious object, sir. They weren't going to give it up.
And now . . . it's gone.'

'Where is it?'

Your kids look at each other, blank.

'Where?' The doctor grabs Mouse's vest; panic floors your boy,
he shakes his head in terror, doesn't know. 'We need it right now,'
the doctor says. 'Who left it behind? Who else is in on this? If
one of you doesn't tell me right now who left it behind I'm going
to deal with each of you one by one. Starting with . . . him.'

Tidge. Your beautiful shining boy. Unfinished business of
course. And doesn't a person's behaviour tell you exactly where
they are spiritually, whether they're rattling and unhinged and
empty or filled with light? You breathe in this little man like
ash and flame and it scalds your throat for this is a person who
once had three hundred killed, as a birthday gift, every two
minutes, in the back of the head; you have heard of it. And
now, and now. Your son's eyes. Eight years old. His whimper.
The pistol at the beautiful plane of his temple you've grazed
so much with your lips.

'Who left it?' The pistol moves closer, harder, your boy sobs. '*Tell* me.'

'It was me.'

His brother steps strongly forward and looks the man straight in the eye.

'I did. I left it.'

'Well, you fool.'

And with the full force of an adult hand Mouse is hit across the face.

He falls back. With a blow to his head. On the punishing edge of the jade desk.

As if heaven itself has sucked in its breath.

Let us love, not in word or speech, but in truth and action.

❧ 137 ❧

your broken little boy
pale as flour on his back and still
so still
so still
legs and arms wrong
then blood. now blood. blood.
from the back of his skull.
slow . . . a single stream

Put on the whole armour of God.

❦ **138** ❧

Noooooooooooooooooooooooooooooo.

From his brother; from his sister.

But louder and longer from someone else.

Pin.

'He was my friend. I *told* you.'

His mouth as indignant as an opera singer's, a web of wet.

Men loved darkness rather than light.

⤜ 139 ⤛

A soldier bursts into the room. 'Sorry, got held up.' Grinning like a little boy. Something under his arm. Everyone looking.

'What is that?' Pin's father.

'A doll.' The soldier laughs. 'The kids had it. It must have dropped on the floor.' He tosses Motl's doll across to the captain, who catches it by a leg, strides across to Mouse, and kicks him.

'Fool,' he hisses, 'idiot.'

As if your world has stopped.

At your boy.

What he has done.

His mad sacrifice.

One shall be taken and the other left.

❦ 140 ❧

Out of the stunned silence softly but gathering force Tidge's wailing comes; it goes on and on, it does not stop; a cry of the most agonising distress. Souls, angry souls, feel close.

'Get out,' the doctor orders the soldiers.

Tidge drops to his brother's crazy enormous impetuous heart and hovers his hand over it, can hardly bear to touch, then lies down next to him as close as he can, breathing him in, and slings his arm over him and cries, 'Mousie,' but a cloud bank shifts across your boy's face; it is going to another place, there is a stately progression from sun into shadow and Soli drops down and lifts his head and cradles its terrible flop. Her other hand finds Mouse's and entwines it in hers, a hanky to her wet face, and Tidge looks up at Pin's father: 'Please return my heart,' says his face, 'which you have just wrenched out with a filthy fist.'

I shall go softly all my years in the bitterness of my soul.

247

❦ 141 ❧

A roaring silence.

Only when he knows does he say that he knows.

∞ 142 ∞

'We need a doctor.' Soli, soft.

'My father is a doctor.' Pin cries. 'Ask him what a noble kind he is. Show us, Dad. Be the hero. I want to see it.'

'I will not let you win this,' Tidge shouts, sweeping up the doll and slipping it under his brother's arm then rising before them half the person he was minutes ago but standing before them someone new, a warrior of his blood. Stripped of all his silliness, grown up. Pin stands strong beside hin, shoulder to shoulder.

> *The fathers have eaten sour grapes*
> *and the children's teeth are set on edge.*

❧ 143 ❧

But your beautiful broken boy. Mouse's pale face, his eyelids shining. Tidge and Soli now cradle his looseness in their arms and breathe him in like a first cigarette, breathe in the sharpness of his slipping but his beautiful face is stopped, the wind picks up, a window slams shut; his eyes flicker under his lids, back and forth, back and forth, as if he's witnessing the most astonishing sight; he doesn't look distressed, he's embracing whatever is ahead, striding strongly into it.

'Come on, dude,' his siblings plead. 'Come on.'

Your wild love, your wild love.

He wakes.

He *wakes*.

'I'm starving. What's to eat?'

> *It is the final proof of God's omnipotence*
> *that he need not exist in order to save us.*

✺ 144 ✺

Four children. Laughing and laughing. A great audacious glee pushing through them.

They try to shut it off but cannot.

It is life.

So much life in this room.

In their hearts.

Pin laughs longest and loudest, he cannot stop. The room is ringing with his clear, unstoppable force and his father is staring at a sound he hasn't heard for so long, at this new son in his life, at the fresh child, *child*, broken out. The wonder of it.

> *Think of this picture as they now travel:*
> *the million candles in the sky lit and singing.*

❧ 145 ❧

'We need a bandage,' Pin says, still laughing.

And so here they are. Father and son standing face-to-face with a great churning in them both. Each poised on the cusp of awareness. Each, unmoving.

'We need a bandage,' Pin repeats. 'You're a doctor.'

Wordlessly it is the father who eventually walks away. He retrieves a first-aid kit from a drawer of his desk. Wordlessly it is he who wraps a bandage around your boy's head. When he is finished he goes to a jade panel and presses his body into it and closes his eyes as if he is trying to press out an enormous weight. An elderly man suddenly. With a ruined kind of brokenness in his face. The stillness of a warrior who has just had a crushing loss, who has never had a defeat of such magnitude in his life. Because it involves the one thing he controlled the most. He has had to surrender, to get his son back, to save the grand plan of his life.

As drops of water eventually fill a pot,
so is an unskilful man eventually filled with cares.

❧ 146 ❧

But Pin has not finished.

'Let them go, Dad.'

His father blinks, slowly, all the winter in his heart back.

'Just let them walk out of here?'

'They're no one. And they've been through enough. Let them off, just this once.'

'Do unto them what they will surely tomorrow do unto us.' But weary now.

'Maybe they'll be so grateful they'll never consider it.'

'Oh yes. It always happens like that.'

'What's happened to you? Who *stole* you?' The boy walks up to his father, firmer, stepping into a new self. 'If you don't let them go I'm walking out of this room and never coming back.'

His father snorts in disbelief.

'I'm so sick of living like this.'

'What about the man downstairs, being interrogated as we speak?'

'Perhaps he was telling the truth. I wanted someone to play with. I dragged them into this. He came in to find them and they all got caught.'

'It's gone too far, son.'

'I will leave you. I will disgrace our house. I've read our holy book. It says to love not to hate and you and your men, you all change the words and turn it into something else.' And without another word Pin turns on his heels in disgust and walks out. An act of glorious, mad, courageous independence and you long to tell Motl of it, to feel the room fill with his air punch because compassion can still be found and he needs to know, he'd lost faith, it was all in his cling on that final night at Salt Cottage as he curled around his children and held them tight, so tight, and didn't want to set them loose, didn't trust the world anymore, had lost hope.

Compassion and tolerance are not a sign of weakness but a sign of strength.

∝ 147 ∾

The doctor storms out after the son and your three children spin to the windows, to the celebratory blue hollering for them to get out.

'Come on,' Soli whispers.

'Quick.' Tidge laughs.

'No,' Mouse says, 'not yet.'

'It's just *there*,' Tidge cries with his arm around his brother's shoulders but Mouse rubs his head and says, 'No,' as if the whole idea hurts. Tidge drops his hand. His brother hasn't stopped them because of his pain, he's stopped them because of something else.

'This isn't the way to do it,' Mouse says. 'It'll only make things worse.'

> *Be truthful, be patient, be generous.*
> *These are the three steps to godliness.*

So. The three of them here. Staying because they have to. Because it can't be just two of them escaping, because no one's being left behind. Waiting in this room of shimmering light as two enormous wills do battle in the corridor outside and as Pin walks through the door his face tells you what you never thought you'd see: he has won.

Brim your heart.

Pin gives them the thumbs up, his eyes dance, Soli runs to the waiting blue. Holds out her palms and laughs, holds them flat to the light; drinks up the sky for it's theirs now, soon, back. The beautiful repairing sun, any moment. The doctor comes into the room and brisks to the desk. He picks up the phone, drumming his fingers impatiently on a book.

'How did you do it? What did you say?' Your children fire questions as the doctor concentrates on his call, a hand shielding his forehead as if holding in an enormous headache.

'I know something I'm not meant to,' Pin sings in a whisper.

'What? What?'

'Something a lot of people want to know. And will pay a lot of money for.'

'*What?*'

'I know where _____ is. The exact location.'

Your children suck in their breaths. Where, exactly, the man at the heart of this endless fear plague is; the puppet master with the sad speaking eyes who has kept their world under his thumb, for years now, by a masterful manipulation of paranoia and mystery and fret, by an audacious sense of grandeur and theatrical cunning, by an unholy lust for death. The world has been searching for him for decades now; it's not known if he's still alive, he's morphed into myth.

'There was a note. A map' – Pin grins – 'in Dad's pocket. I found it by mistake. I copied it. I was looking for Tic Tacs. And I've said to Dad that I've told several people who I trust where I've hidden the information. They don't know exactly what's in the envelope, but it's somewhere in this building, and it's to be sent on my behalf if ever I give the signal. Or if something ever happens to me. And I've just told Dad that if you're set free – *all* of you, the four of you' — your children gasp in joy — 'yes, *every* one' – he pokes Tidge playfully in the chest – 'then he can have his envelope back. You're nothing to him. And the information is priceless.'

Pin smiles a smile that in an afternoon has grown up. 'The things I do to get you off. *And* those crazy siblings of yours.' He steps back and assesses them. 'I'm not sure it's worth it, you know.'

You want to hold that boy for a very long time, hold him and hold him, in this crackly air, for he has sanctified himself.

A faithful friend is the medicine of life.

∽ 149 ∾

Pin asks his father if they can have one last play in their room.

The man begins to speak but stops, a hostage now to a son who knows too much. 'But I'm coming with you,' he says, 'I want to check that room out.'

So. There those children are, abreast, walking tall down that corridor into four new lives. Did they call themselves alive in the past? It is nothing compared to now. Their hearts are like windsocks in a stiff breeze, filled up, and you feel stunned by all of this. You have learned astonishment today; from your children, from their friend, from everything that's gone on. Getting softer and looser by the minute, like an anemone sprung into life by the water's caress, rescued by forgiveness and brimming with light. They are better than you. They teach you so much.

They take the lift to the basement. Miss Jude Pickering the Third gives not a flicker of recognition, but as your children step out she brushes Mouse's back, once, in fleeting warmth. It's all he gets but it's enough. She's in the secret, silent loop, just as B is, and so many unseen others in this fragile world and even, perhaps, your Motl, you will never know, it doesn't matter now. For you have made your choice and you are strong with it. You are so in love with life.

They walk tall to the room that has imprisoned them for so many days, feeling straighter and stronger with every step they take. Relief is turning them all zippy and giggly, they can hardly contain their energy; soon they'll be flooding their lungs with sun, soon. And you must let them go now, you must turn from this, striding into a darkness that is luminous, marinated in love and at peace.

Friend, go up higher.

❧ 150 ❧

Pin's father checks behind curtains and whips the cover from the bed. Begins to open the cupboard with Mouse's quilt of words within it. Your boy's face is as white as flour. The man's pocket rings. He takes out a phone, concentrating on the call and missing entirely the meticulous chronicle of their life in this place. The man turns to a corner of the room deep in talk. Mouse flops on the bed, arms spread, and smiles in enormous relief.

Suddenly, slogged by tired. All four of them. There's still much to be done. Mouse looks at the cupboard; his words have to be tidied for a start. He hates the thought of leaving it unfinished: 'Write as if you're dying,' you'd said with a laugh once, 'believe me, it works.' He slips out his father's pen and gazes at it as if it's a sword to be carried through the biggest battles of his life. Each of your children takes a last look around. Part of them will be left behind in this place but three new people are stepping out, uncurling their pale backs, grown tall, spined up. Outside a wind has come, it's whipping up a flurry of leaves and dust, rattling windows and snatching hats, moving the world on. Calling your children into the tall happy light and they're more than ready now to be among it, your three bouncy puppies, running and lolloping at all the green shoots.

Look at Soli. Shining. Retrieving your scrap of kitchen towel from inside her pillow case, holding it to her face and breathing it in deep, your gardenia perfume still faintly upon it. Look at

Tidge. Clutching his father's doll as he reaches under the bed to collect your old key to whatever they want, clutching his doll like he'll never give him up. He can't reach. Pin drops to his knees, gets it, just: 'Bingo,' he says, handing the key across. Your boy holds it to his lips and chuckles his thanks, chuckles and chuckles, they both do, can't stop. The others join in, joy roguish through each of them and the wonder intensifies. At all of this, all that has happened in this place. Because it feels like you've been bulleted into living and the world surprises you still and that gives you hope. You've witnessed something rescuing here. Grace. Which can change everything in an instant. Release hearts.

They'll be all right, they'll be all right.

A serious house on serious earth it is.

∞ 151 ∞

The doctor drifts into the corridor, lured away by the importance of his call. Mouse calls Pin across. Opens the cupboard door, trust now brimming his heart.

'Wow,' his friend whispers, running his hand over all the words like a jockey appreciating a horse.

'You can read it all when we're long gone from here. Will you look after it for me?'

'Of course.'

'My dad told me to do it,' Mouse says. 'He said that telling the truth gives you this weird kind of calmness among all the craziness. It's been like my daily glass of whisky, I guess.' They both laugh. 'Now there's just one more thing I've got to do.' He slips inside. 'To finish it off. I just need a moment.'

This. (Hang on. Soli's yelling out. 'What, sister dear?' 'Thank you, Mr.' 'For what?' 'For being so grown up. For helping out. You write that down.' Well, if I must, I must.)

Whistling away in there, and your heart is filled with it.

Now where I was I? Oh yeah. Imagine this. I'm running down to the beach at Salt Cottage and stripping off and getting sand all over me and cleaning myself with it and RUBBING THIS WHOLE EPISODE OUT. Kaput. And then I'll just be quiet for a bit. No words. I want to lose talk for a while, and all the writing, and just stand there and let the sea and the sun and the wind blow it clean out of me. And rest. God yeah, that. Ahead feels like this big empty house that's warm with light and waiting and ready to be filled up. It's CLOSE! YIPPEE!!

So to this. The photo of their football, the last thing left from the memory box. Curling on its bit of toothpaste and Mouse wants it with him, wherever they're off to next, so much. He hovers his fingers over it, can hardly bear to touch, hovers, can't quite abandon it.

No. I'll leave it. For you. For us.
These things are happening. CAN ANYONE HEAR US?

Love does not dominate; it cultivates.

∞ 152 ∞

The Last

Reality now, this irreversibility. You know what is wanted, you have made your choice; you have to open your heart, surrender, to move from this limbo into the light. And so this. Your final testament, your conclusion, for you are the last one left with the key to unlock Project Indigo. You understand what is required of you now. You will see your children again if you do what is best for the research, you will see your husband again if you do what is best for the research, you will leave this room if you do what is best for the research. They have given you a sheaf of paper and a pen, and this testimony you have sewn them and sewn them in response is what is needed, required, now. They will get nothing else. You have learned the rightful resonances of the word sacrifice. You have learned a lot. All their roaring words, yes, in all their books; but now *your* roaring words. This manuscript, this final testament, will find its way to a good place, you are sure of that. You have made your choice and you are strong with it. It is time to go. You are not afraid. Your family will be alright, your children are in safe hands. This room is lumen now. What you believe in is all you have left.

Nothing evolves us like love.

Chapter Lessons:
Sources

Lesson 1: Hafiz (fourteenth-century Persian poet)
2: The Bible
3: The Koran
4: The Bible
5: Robert Burton
6: Samuel Johnson
7: The Bible
8: The Koran
9: Gotama Buddha
10: The Bible
11: Hafiz
12: The Koran
13: The Koran
14: The Koran
15: Hafiz
16: Fiona Omeenyo (Australian Aboriginal artist)
17: The Bible
18: Buddha
19: Confucianist Scriptures: The Shih King
20: Buddha
21: Hafiz
22: Aristotle
23: The Bible

24: The Koran
25: Buddha
26: Dalai Lama
27: Buddha
28: Confucianist Scriptures: Lamentation
29: Buddha
30: The Koran
31: The Bible
32: Hafiz
33: Hafiz
34: The Bible
35: The Bible
36: The Bible
37: The Bible
38: Oliver Cromwell
39: The Koran
40: Buddha
41: The Bible
42: The Bible
43: The Koran
44: The Bible
45: Hafiz
46: Buddha
47: Hafiz
48: Hafiz
49: Dalai Lama
50: The Rig Veda Samhita
51: Hafiz
52: The Bible
53: Hafiz
54: Hafiz
55: Iris Murdoch
56: Hafiz
57: The Koran

58: Buddha
59: Hafiz
60: The Bible
61: Hafiz
62: The Bible
63: Buddha
64: The Bible
65: Buddha
66: Buddha
67: C.S. Lewis
68: Confucianist Scriptures: The Li Ki
69: The Bible
70: Buddha
71: The Koran
72: The Bible
73: Hafiz
74: Buddha
75: The Bible
76: The Bible
77: The Bible
78: Hafiz
79: Buddha
80: The Koran
81: The Bible
82: Buddha
83: Hafiz
84: The Koran
85: Patrick White
86: The Bible
87: Dalai Lama
88: Ella Wheeler Wilcox
89: Buddha
90: The Koran
91: The Koran

92: Hafiz
93: The Bible
94: The Bible
95: The Bible
96: Cicero
97: The Bible
98: Willa Cather
99: The Bible
100: Benjamin Disraeli
101: Hafiz
102: Matthew Arnold
103: The Bible
104: The Bible
105: The Bible
106: Sri Ramakrishna
107: The Bible
108: The Koran
109: The Bible
110: The Bible
111: Robert Browning
112: Buddha
113: Buddha
114: The Bible
115: The Bible
116: The Koran
117: Dalai Lama
118: The Bible
119: The Koran
120: Oscar Wilde
121: Buddha
122: Hafiz
123: R.S. Thomas
124: The Bible
125: The Bible